Celtic Tales of Terror

Celtic Tales of Terror

Edited by Mairtin O'Griofa

Illustrated by Marlene Ekman

A Sterling/Main Street Book
Sterling Publishing Co., Inc.   New York

Library of Congress Cataloging-in-Publication Data.

Celtic tales of terror / edited by Mairtin O'Griofa
    p. cm.
"A Sterling/Main Street book."
ISBN 0-8069-0868-8
1. Horror tales, English—Irish authors. 2. Ireland—Fiction.
I. O'Griofa, Mairtin.
PR8876.5.H67C45 1994
823'.08738089415—dc20   94-3394
                                                  CIP

Designed by John Murphy
Typeset by Upper Case Limited, Cork, Ireland.

10   9   8   7   6   5   4   3   2   1

A Sterling/Main Street Book

Published in 1994 by Sterling Publishing Company, Inc.
387 Park Avenue South, New York, N.Y. 10016
© 1994 by Sterling Publishing Company, Inc.
Distributed in Canada by Sterling Publishing
c/o Canadian Manda Group, One Atlantic Avenue, Suite 105
Toronto, Ontario, Canada M6K 3E7
Distributed in Great Britain and Europe by Cassell PLC
Villiers House, 41/47 Strand, London WC2N 5JE, England
Distributed in Australia by Capricorn Link (Australia) Pty Ltd.
P.O. Box 6651, Baulkham Hills, Business Centre, NSW 2153,
Australia

Manufactured in the United States of America
All rights reserved

ISBN 0-8069-0868-8

Contents

Introduction	7
Wicked Captain Walshawe *by Joseph Sheridan Le Fanu*	9
The Witch Hare *from Dublin University Magazine (1839)*	23
Donald and His Neighbors *Traditional*	35
A Play-House in the Waste *by George Moore*	40
The Legend of Knockgrafton *by Thomas Crofton Croker*	53
The Crucifixion of the Outcast *by W. B. Yeats*	60
Daniel O'Rourke *by Thomas Crofton Croker*	69
The Eyes of the Dead *by Daniel Corkery*	78
The Three Wishes *by William Carleton*	91
Hertford O'Donnell's Warning *by Charlotte Riddell*	119
Index	144

Introduction

THE LITERATURE of the Irish Celts has always reflected a preternatural fear of the unknown and an unshakable belief in the supernatural, characteristic of both ancient and modern fiction. *Celtic Tales of Terror* brings together ten of the best stories of the bizarre, works that place an instinctive eye on the forces of the unknown. The Irish frequently leaven their vision of the dark side with humor, and two of the stories—"Daniel O'Rourke" and "The Three Wishes"—alternately amuse and disturb. The remaining nine make the unreal real and the known all too familiar. The stories are by the following authors:

Joseph Sheridan Le Fanu (1814-1873), while known today primarily for his pioneering tales of ratiocination, remains paramount as one of the finest masters of supernatural fiction. "Wicked Captain Walshawe," a tale of macabre terror, first appeared in *Dublin University Magazine*, of which "the Irish Poe" was editor and owner.

George Moore (1852-1933), considered by many to be the creator of the modern Irish short story, was influenced by the work of Emile Zola and combined in his works a thorough knowledge of Irish life and superstitions and social criticism of rural poverty. "A Play-House in the Waste," his tale of "a white thing gliding," is from Moore's collection of stories, *An Untilled Field*.

Thomas Crofton Croker (1798-1854), author of *Fairy Legends and Traditions of the South of Ireland,* is one of the most distinguished of all Irish folklore collectors. "The Legend of Knockgrafton" and "Daniel O'Rourke," both taken from that multivolumed book, are fantastic flights of the imagination, the former as moralistic as it is fanciful and the latter merging terror and humor.

W. B. Yeats (1865-1939) is acknowledged as Ireland's greatest poet. "The Crucifixion of the Outcast," published in 1898, reflects both his early interest in Irish folklore and his love of Celtic legend. It is a tale of terror, possibly influenced by Poe, that may be read as an allegory of his countrymen's philistinic rejection of Irish poetry and drama.

Daniel Corkery (1878-1964), influenced by Russian literature, envisioned an Irish literature as powerful as the Russian and deriving from everyday Irish life. "The Eyes of the Dead," a story of the living dead, is from his collection, *The Stormy Hills*.

William Carleton (1794-1869), author of *Traits and Stories of the Irish Peasantry*, his most famous work, refashioned the tales he had heard from native story-tellers into literature of the highest order. "The Three Wishes" is a tale in which the Devil, despite his otherworldly powers, is seen in human terms. If ever a Celtic tale of terror could be called a comic masterpiece, this is it.

Charlotte Riddell (1832-1906), born in Ireland but resident for most of her life in London, was editor and co-proprietor of *St. James's Magazine* and a prolific Victorian novelist. "Hertford O'Donnell's Warning," a terrifying tale of an Irish Banshee's appearance across the Irish Sea in England, reflects the blending of her Celtic origin with her English adoption.

Wicked Captain Walshawe
Joseph Sheridan Le Fanu

A VERY ODD thing happened to my uncle, Mr. Watson, of Haddlestone; and to enable you to understand it, I must begin at the beginning.

In the year 1822, Mr. James Walshawe, more commonly known as Captain Walshawe, died at the age of eighty-one years. The Captain in his early days, and so long as health and strength permitted, was a scamp of the active, intriguing sort; and spent his days and nights in sowing wild oats, of which he seemed to have an inexhaustible stock.

Captain Walshawe was very well known in the neighborhood of Wauling, and very generally avoided there. He had quitted the service in 1766, at the age of twenty-five, immediately previous to which period his debts had grown so troublesome that he was induced to extricate himself by running away with and marrying an heiress. He was quartered in Ireland, at Clonmel, where was a nunnery, in which, as pensioner, resided Miss O'Neill, or as she was called in the country, Peg O'Neill, the heiress.

Her situation was the only ingredient of romance in the affair, for the young lady was decidedly plain, though good-humored looking, with that style of features which is termed potato; and in figure she was a little too plump, and rather short. But she was impressible; and the handsome young English lieutenant was too much for her monastic tendencies, and she eloped. They took up their abode at Wauling, in Lancashire.

Here the Captain amused himself after his fashion, sometimes running up, of course, on business to London. He spent her income, frightened her out of her wits, with oath and threats, and broke her heart.

Latterly she shut herself up pretty nearly altogether in her room. She had an old, rather grim, Irish servant-woman in attendance, Molly Doyle. This domestic was lean and religious, and the Captain knew instinctively she hated him; and he hated her in return, and often threatened to put her out of the house, and sometimes even to kick her out of the window.

Years passed away, and old Molly Doyle remained still in her original position. Perhaps he thought that there must be somebody there, and that she was not, after all, very likely to change for the better.

He tolerated another intrusion, too and thought himself a paragon of patience and easy good-nature for so doing. A Roman Catholic clergyman, in long black frock, with a low standing collar, and a little white muslin fillet round his neck—tall, sallow, with blue chin, and dark steady eyes—used to glide up and down the stairs, and through the passages; and the Captain sometimes met him in one place and sometimes in another. But by a caprice incident to such tempers he treated this cleric exceptionally, and even with a surly sort of courtesy, though he grumbled about his visits behind his back.

Well, the time came at last, when poor Peg O'Neill—in an evil hour Mrs. James Walshawe—must cry, and quake, and pray her last. The doctor came from Penlynden, and was just as vague as usual, but more gloomy, and for about a week came and went oftener. The cleric in the long black frock was also daily there. And at last came that last sacrament in the gates of death, when the sinner is traversing those dread steps and never can be retraced.

The Captain drank a great deal of brandy and water that night, and called in Farmer Dobbs, for want of better company, to drink with him; and told him all his grievances, and how happy he and the poor lady upstairs might have been had it not been for liars, and pick-thanks, and tale-bearers. and the like, who came between them—meaning Molly Doyle—whom, as he waxed eloquent over his liquor, he came to curse and rail at by name, with more than his accustomed freedom. And he described his own natural character and amiability in such moving terms that he wept maudlin tears of sensibility over his theme; and when Dobbs was gone, drank some more grog, and took to railing and cursing again by himself; and then mounted the stairs unsteadily to see "what the devil Doyle and the other old witches were about in poor Peg's room."

When he pushed open the door, he found some half-dozen crones, chiefly Irish, from the neighboring town of Hackleton, sitting over tea and snuff, etc., with candles lighted round the corpse, which was arrayed in a strangely cut robe of brown serge. She had secretly belonged to some order—I think the Carmelite, but 1 am not certain—and wore the habit in her coffin.

"What the d ____ are you doing with my wife?" cried the Captain, rather thickly. "How dare you dress her up in this—trumpery, you—you cheating old witch; and what's that candle doing in her hand?"

I think he was a little startled, for the spectacle was grisly enough. The dead lady was arrayed in this strange brown robe, and in her rigid fingers, as in a socket, with the large wooden beads and cross wound round it, burned a wax candle, shedding its white light over the sharp features of the corpse. Molly Doyle was not to be put down by the Captain, whom she hated, and accordingly, in her phrase, "he got as good as he gave." And the Captain's wrath waxed fiercer, and he plucked the wax taper from the dead hand, and was on the point of flinging it at the old serving-woman's head.

"The holy candle, you sinner!" cried she.

"I've a mind to make you eat it, you beast," cried the Captain.

But I think he had not known before what it was, for he subsided, a little sulkily, and he stuffed his hand with the candle (quite extinct by this time) into his pocket, and said he:

"You know devilish well you had no business going on with y-y-your d—— witchcraft about my poor wife, without my leave—you do—and you'll please to take off that d—— brown pinafore, and get her decently into her coffin, and I'll pitch your devil's waxlight into the sink."

And the Captain stalked out of the room.

"An' now her poor sowl's in prison, you wretch, be the mains o' ye; an' may your own be shut into the wick o' that same candle, till it's burned out, ye savage."

"I'd have you ducked for a witch, for twopence," roared the Captain up the staircase, with his hand on the banisters, standing on the lobby. But the door of the chamber of death clapped angrily, and he went down to the parlor, where he examined the holy candle for a while with a tipsy gravity, and then with something of that reverential feeling for the symbolic, which is not uncommon in rakes and scamps, he thoughtfully locked it up in a press, where were accumulated all sorts of obsolete rubbish—soiled packs of cards, disused tobacco-pipes, broken powder-flasks, his military sword, and a dusty bundle of the *Flash Songster* and other questionable literature.

Captain Walshawe reigned alone for many years at Wauling. He was too shrewd and too experienced by this time to run violently down the steep hill that leads to ruin. Forty years acted forcibly upon the gay Captain Walshawe. Gout supervened, and was no more conducive to temper than to enjoyment, and made his elegant hands lumpy at all the small joints, and turned them slowly into crippled claws. He grew stout when his exercise was interfered with, and ultimately almost corpulent. He suffered from what Mr. Holloway calls "bad legs," and was wheeled about in a great leathernback chair, and his infirmities went on accumulating with his years.

I am sorry to say, I never heard that he repented, or turned his thoughts seriously to the future. On the contrary, his talk grew fouler, and his fun ran upon his favorite sins, and his temper waxed more truculent. But he did not sink into dotage. Considering his bodily infirmities, his energies and his malignities, which were many and active, were marvelously little abated by time.

It was a peculiarity of Captain Walshawe, that he, by this time, hated nearly everybody. My uncle, Mr. Watson, of Haddlestone, was cousin to the Captain, and his heir at law. But my uncle had lent him money on mortgage of his estates and there had been a treaty to sell, and terms and a price were agreed upon, in "articles" which the lawyers said were still in force.

I think the ill-conditioned Captain bore him a grudge for being richer that he, and would have liked to do him an ill turn. But it did not lie in his way; at least while he was living.

My Uncle Watson was a Methodist, and what they call a "class leader," and, on the whole, a very good man. He was now near fifty—grave, as beseemed his profession—somewhat dry and a little severe, perhaps—but a just man.

A letter from the Penlynden doctor reached him at Haddlestone, announcing the death of the wicked old Captain; and suggesting his attendance at the funeral and the expediency of his being on the spot to look after things at Wauling. The reasonableness of this striking my good uncle, he made his journey to the old house in Lancashire incontinently, and reached it in time for the funeral.

The day turning out awfully rainy and tempestuous, my uncle persuaded the doctor and the attorney to remain for the night at Wauling.

There was no will—the attorney was sure of that—for the Captain's enmities were perpetually shifting, and he could never quite make up his mind as to how best to give effect to a malignity whose direction was being constantly modified.

Search being made, no will was found. The papers, indeed, were all right, with one important exception: the leases were nowhere to be seen. My uncle searched strenuously. The attorney was at his elbow, and the doctor helped with a suggestion now and then. The old serving man seemed an honest, deaf creature, and really knew nothing.

My uncle Watson was very much perturbed. He fancied—but this possibly was only fancy—that he had detected for a moment a queer look in the attorney's face, and from that instant it became fixed in his mind that he knew all about the leases. Mr. Watson expounded that evening in the parlor to the doctor, the attorney and the deaf servant.

Ananias and Sapphira figured in the foreground, and the awful nature of fraud and theft, or tampering in any wise with the plain rule of honesty in matters pertaining to estates, etc., were pointedly dwelt upon; and then came a long and strenuous prayer, in which he entreated with fervor and aplomb that the hard heart of the sinner who had abstracted the leases might be softened or broken in such a way as to lead to their restitution; or that if he continued reserved and contumacious, it might at least be the will of Heaven to bring him to public justice and the documents to light. The fact is, that he was praying all this time at the attorney.

When these religious exercises were over, the visitors retired to their rooms, and my Uncle Watson wrote two or three pressing letters by the fire. When his task was done, it had grown late; the candles were flaring in their sockets, and all in bed, and I suppose, asleep, but he.

The fire was nearly out, he chilly, and the flame of the candles throbbing strangely in their sockets shed alternate glare and shadow round the old wainscoted room and its quaint furniture. Outside were the wild thunder and piping of the storm, and the rattling of distant windows sounded through the passages, and down the stairs, like angry people astir in the house.

My Uncle Watson belonged to a sect who by no means reject the supernatural, and whose founder, on the contrary, has sanctioned ghosts in the most emphatic way. He was glad, therefore, to remember, that in prosecuting his search that day, he had seen some six inches of wax candle in the press in the parlor; for he had no fancy to be overtaken by darkness in his present situation.

He had no time to lose; and taking the bunch of keys of which he was now master—he soon fitted the lock and secured the candle—a treasure in his circumstances; and lighting it, he stuffed it into the socket of one of the expiring candles, and extinguishing the other, he looked round the room in the steady light, reassured. At the same moment an unusually violent gust of the storm blew a handful of gravel against the parlor window with a sharp rattle that startled him in the midst of the roar and hubbub; and the fiame of the candle itself was agitated by the air.

My uncle walked up to bed, guarding his candle with his hand, for the lobby windows were rattling furiously and he disliked the idea of being left in the dark more than ever.

His bedroom was comfortable, though old-fashioned. He shut and bolted the door. There was a tall looking-glass opposite the foot of his four-poster on the dressing-table between the windows. He tried to make the curtains meet, but they would not draw.

He turned the face of the mirror away, therefore, so that its back was presented to the bed, pulled the curtains together, and placed a chair against them to prevent their falling open again. There was a good fire, and a reinforcement of round coal and wood inside the fender. So he piled it up to ensure a cheerful blaze through the night, and placing a little black mahogany table, with the legs of a Satyr, beside the bed, and his candle upon it, he got between the sheets, and laid his red nightcapped head upon the pillow, and disposed himself to sleep.

The first thing that made him uncomfortable was a sound at the foot of his bed, quite distinct in a momentary lull of the storm. It was only the gentle rustle and rush of the curtains which fell open again; and as his eyes opened, he saw them resuming their prependicular dependence, and sat up in his bed almost expecting to see something uncanny in the aperture.

There was nothing, however, but the dressing-table and other dark furniture, and the window-curtains faintly undulating in the violence of the storm. He did not care to get up, therefore—the fire being bright and cheery—to replace the curtains by a chair, in the position in which he had left them, anticipating possibly a new recurrence of the relapse which had startled him from his incipient doze.

So he got to sleep in a little while again, but he was disturbed by a sound, as he fancied, at the table on which stood the candle. He could not say what it was, only that he wakened with a start, and lying so in some amaze, he did distinctly hear a sound which startled him a good deal, though there was nothing necessarily supernatural in it.

He described it as resembling what would occur if you fancied a thinnish table-leaf, with a convex warp in it, depressed the reverse way, and suddenly with a string recovering its natural convexity. It was a loud, sudden thump, which made the heavy candlestick jump, and there was an end except that my uncle did not get again into a doze for ten minutes at least.

The next time he awoke it was in that odd, serene way that sometimes occurs. We open our eyes, we know not why, quite placidly, and are on the instant wide awake. He had had a nap of some duration this time, for his candle-flame was fluttering and flaring *in articulo*, in the silver socket. But the fire was still bright and cheery, so he popped the extinguisher on the socket, and almost at the same time there came a tap at his door, and a sort of crescendo "hush-sh-sh!" Once more my uncle was sitting up, scared and perturbed in his bed.

He recollected, however, that he had bolted his door; and such inveterate materialists are we in the midst of our spiritualism, that this reassured him, and he breathed a deep sigh, and began to grow tranquil. But after a rest of a minute of two, there came a louder and sharper knock at his door; so that instinctively he called out: "Who's there?" in a loud, stern key. There was no sort of response, however.

The nervous effect of the start subsided; and after a while he lay down with his back turned towards that side of the bed at which was the door, and his face towards the table on which stood the massive old candlestick, capped with its extinguisher, and in that position he closed his eyes. But sleep would not revisit them. All blinds of queer fancies began to trouble him—some of them I remember.

He felt the point of a finger, he averred, pressed most distinctly on the tip of his great toe, as if a living hand were between his sheets, and rnaking a sort of signal of attention or silence. Then again he felt something as large as a rat make a sudden bounce in thc middle of his bolster, just under his head.

Then a voice said: "Oh!" very gently, close at the back of his head. All these things he felt certain of, and yet investigation led to nothing. He felt odd little cramps stealing now and then about him, and then, on a sudden, the middle finger of his right hand was plucked backwards, with a light playful jerk that frightened him awfully.

Meanwhile the storm kept singing and howling and ha-ha-hooing hoarsely among the limbs of the old trees and the chimney-pots; and my Uncle Watson, although he prayed and meditated as was his wont when he lay awake, felt his heart throb steadily, and sometimes thought he was beset with evil spirits, and at others that he was in the early stages of a fever.

He resolutely slept with his eyes closed however, and, like St. Paul's shipwrecked companions, wished for the day. At last another little doze seems to have stolen upon his senses, for he awoke quietly and completely as before—opening his eyes all at once, and seeing everything as if he had not slept for a moment.

The fire was still blazing redly—nothing uncertain in the

light—the massive silver candlestick, topped with its tall extinguisher, stood on the center of the black mahogany table as before; and, looking by what seemed a sort of accident to the apex of this, he beheld something which made him quite misdoubt the evidence of his eyes.

He saw the extinguisher lifted by a tiny hand from beneath, and a small human face, no bigger than a thumb-nail, with nicely proportioned features, peep from beneath it. In this Lilliputian countenance was such a ghastly consternation as horrified my uncle unspeakably.

Out came a little foot then and there, and a pair of wee legs, in short silk stockings and buckled shoes, then the rest of the figure; and, with the arrns holding about the socket, the little legs stretched and stretched, hanging about the stem of the candlestick till the feet reached the base, and so down the Satyr-like leg of the table, till they reached the floor, extending elastically, and strangely enlarging in all proportions as they approached the ground, where the feet and buckles were those of a well-shaped, full-grown man, and the figure tapering upwards until it dwindled to its original fairy dimensions at the top, like an object seen in some strangely curved mirror.

Standing upon the floor he expanded, my amazed uncle could not tell how, into his proper proportions; and stood pretty nearly in profile at the bedside, a handsome and elegantly shaped young man, in a bygone military costume, with a small laced, three-cocked hat and plurne on his head, but looking like a man going to be hanged—in unspeakable despair.

He stepped lightly to the hearth, and turned for a few seconds very dejectedly with his back towards the bed and the mantlepiece, and he saw the hilt of his rapier glittering in the firelight; and then walking across the room, he placed himself at the dressing table visible through the divided curtains at the foot of the bed. The fire was still blazing so brightly that my uncle saw him as distinctly as if half a dozen candles were burning.

The looking-glass was an old-fashioned piece of furniture, and had a drawer beneath it. My uncle had searched it carefully for the papers in the daytime; but the silent figure pulled the drawer quite out, pressed a spring at the side, disclosing a false receptacle behind it, and from this he drew a parcel of papers tied together with pink tape.

All this time my uncle was staring at him in a horrified state, neither winking or breathing and the apparition had not once given the smallest intimation of consciousness that a living person was in the same room. But now, for the first time, it turned its livid stare full upn my uncle with a hateful smile of significance, lifting up the little parcel of papers between his slender finger and thumb.

Then he made a long, cunning wink at him and seemed to blow out one of his checks in a burlesque grimace, which, but for the horrific circumstances, would have been ludicrous. My uncle could not tell whether this was really an intentional distortion or only one of those horrid ripples and deflections which were constantly disturbing the proportions of the figure, as if it were seen through some unequal and perverting medium.

The figure now approached the bed, seeming to grow exhausted and malignant as it did so. My uncle's terror nearly culminated at this point for he believed it was drawing near him with an evil purpose. But it was not so; for the soldier, over whom twenty years seemed to have passed in his brief transit to the dressing-table and back again, threw himself into a great high-backed armchair of stuffed leather at the far side of the fire, and placed his heels on the fender.

His feet and legs seemed indistinctly to swell, and swathings showed themselves round them, and they grew into something enormous, and the upper figure swayed and shaped itself into corresponding proportions, a great mass of corpulence, with a cadaverous and malignant face, and the furrows of a great old age, and colorless glassy eyes; and with these changes, which came indefinitely but rapidly as those of a sunset cloud, the fine regimentals faded away, and a loose, grey, woolen drapery, somehow, was there in its stead; and all seemed to be stained and rotten, for swarms of worms seemed creeping in and out, while the figure grew paler and paler, till my uncle, who liked his pipe, and employed the simile naturally, said the whole effigy grew to the color of tobacco ashes, and the clusters of worms into little wriggling knots of sparks such as we see running over the residium of a burnt sheet of paper.

And so with the strong draft caused by the fire, and the current of air from the window, which was rattling in the storm, the feet seemed to be drawn into the fireplace, and the whole figure, light as ashes, floated away with them and disappeared with a whisk up the capacious old chimney.

It seemed to my uncle that the fire suddenly darkened and the air grew icy cold, and there came an awful roar and riot of tempest, which shook the old house from top to base, and sounded like the yelling of a blood-thirsty mob on receiving a new and long-expected victim.

Good Uncle Watson used to say: "I have been in many situations of fear and danger in the course of my life, but never did I pray with so much agony before or since; for then, as now, it was clear beyond a cavil that I had actually beheld the phantom of an evil spirit."

Now there are two curious circumstances to be observed on this relation of my uncle's, who was, as I have said, a perfectly veracious man.

First: The wax candle which he took from the press in the

parlor and burnt at his bedside on that horrible night was unquestionably, according to the testimony of the old deaf servant, who had been fifty years at Wauling, that identical piece of "holy candle" which had stood in the fingers of the poor lady's corpse, and concerning which the old Irish crone, long since dead, had delivered the curious curse I have mentioned against the Captain.

Secondly: Behind the drawer under the looking-glass, he did actually discover a second but secret drawer, in which were concealed the identical papers which he had suspected the attorney of having made away with. There were circumstances too, afterward disclosed, which convinced my uncle that the old man had deposited them there preparatory to burning them, which he had nearly made up his mind to do.

Now, a very remarkable ingredient in this tale of my Uncle Watson was this, that so far as my father, who had never seen Captain Walshawe in the course of his life, could gather, the phantom had exhibited a horrible and grotesque, but unmistakable, resemblance to that defunct scamp in the various stages of his long life.

Wauling was sold in the year 1837, and the old house shortly after pulled down, and a new one built nearer to the river. I often wondered whether it was rumored to be haunted, and, if so, what stories were current about it. It was a commodious and staunch old house, and withall rather handsome; and its demolition was certainly suspicious.

The Witch Hare
Dublin University Magazine (1839)

ABOUT the commencement of the last century there lived in the vicinity of the once famous village of Aghavoe a wealthy farmer, named Bryan Costigan. This man kept an extensive dairy and a great many milch cows and every year made considerable sums by the sale of milk and butter. The luxuriance of the pasture lands in this neighborhood has always been proverbial; and, consequently, Bryan's cows were the finest and most productive in the country, and his milk and butter the richest and sweetest, and brought the highest price at every market at which he ordered these articles for sale.

Things continued to go on thus prosperously with Bryan Costigan, when, one season all at once, he found his cattle declining in appearance, and his dairy almost entirely profitless. Bryan, at first, attributed this change to the weather, or some such cause, but soon found or fancied reasons to assign it to a far different source. The cows, without any visible disorder, daily declined, and were scarcely able to crawl about on their pasture; many of them, instead of milk, gave nothing but blood; and the scanty quantity of milk which some of them continued to supply was so bitter that even the pigs would not drink it; while the butter which it produced was of such a bad quality, and stunk so horribly, that the very dogs would not eat it. Bryan applied for remedies to all the quacks and "fairy-women" in the country—but in vain. Many of the imposters declared that the mysterious malady in his cattle went beyond *their* skill; while others, although they found no difficulty in tracing it to superhuman agency, declared that they had no control in the matter, as the charm under the influence of which his property was made away with, was too powerful to be dissolved by anything less than the special interposition of Divine Providence. The poor farmer became almost distracted; he saw ruin staring him in the face; yet what was he to do? Sell his cattle and purchase others! No; that was out of the question, as they looked so miserable and emaciated that no one would even take them as a present, while it was also impossible to sell to a butcher, as the flesh of one which he killed for his own family was as black as a coal, and stunk like any putrid carrion.

The unfortunate man was thus completely bewildered. He knew not what to do; he became moody and stupid; his sleep forsook him by night, and all day he wandered about the fields, among his "fairy-stricken" cattle like a maniac.

Affairs continued in this plight, when one very sultry evening in the latter days of July, Bryan Costigan's wife was sitting at her own door, spinning at her wheel, in a very gloomy and agitated state of mind. Happening to look down the narrow green lane which led from the high road to her cabin, she espied a little old woman barefoot, and enveloped in an old scarlet cloak, approaching slowly, with the aid of a crutch which she carried in one hand, and a cane or walking-stick in the other. The farmer's wife felt glad at seeing the odd-looking stranger; she smiled, and yet she knew not why, as she neared the house. A vague and indefinable feeling of pleasure crowded on her imagination; and, as the old woman gained the threshold, she bade her "welcome" with a warmth which plainly told that her lips gave utterance but to the genuine feelings of her heart.

"God bless this good house and all belonging to it," said the stranger as she entered.

"God save you kindly, and you are welcome, whoever you are," replied Mrs. Costigan.

"Hem, I thought so," said the old woman with a significant grin. "I thought so, or I wouldn't trouble you."

The farmer's wife ran, and placed a chair near the fire for the stranger, but she refused, and sat on the ground near where Mrs. Costigan had been spinning. Mrs. Costigan had now time to survey the old hag's person minutely. She appeared of great age; her countenance was extremely ugly and repulsive; her skin was rough and deeply embrowned as if from long exposure to the effects of some tropical climate; her forehead was low, narrow, and indented with a thousand wrinkles; her long gray hair fell in matted elf-locks from beneath a white linen skull cap; her eyes were bleared, bloodsotten, and obliquely set in their sockets, and her voice was croaking, tremulous, and, at times, partially inarticulate. As she squatted on the floor, she looked round the house with an inquisitive gaze; she peered pryingly from corner to corner, with an earnestness of look, as if she had the faculty, like the Argonaut of old, to see through the very depths of the earth, while Mrs. C. kept watching her motions with mingled feelings of curiosity, awe, and pleasure.

"Mrs.," said the old woman, at length breaking silence, "I am dry with the heat of the day; can you give me a drink?"

"Alas!" replied the farmer's wife, "I have no drink to offer you except water, else you would have no occasion to ask me for it."

"Are you not the owner of the cattle I see yonder?" said the old hag, with a tone of voice and manner of gesticulation which plainly indicated her foreknowledge of the fact.

Mrs. Costigan replied in the affirmative, and briefly related to her every circumstance connected with the affair, while the old woman still remained silent, but shook her gray head repeatedly and still continued gazing round the house with an air of importance and self-sufficiency.

When Mrs. C. had ended, the old hag remained a while as if in a deep reverie; at length she said:

"Have you any of the milk in the house?"

"I have," replied the other.

"Show me some of it."

She filled a jug from a vessel and handed it to the old sybil, who smelled it, then tasted it, and spat out what she had taken on the floor.

"Where is your husband?" she asked.

"Out in the fields," was the reply.

"I must see him."

A messenger was despatched for Bryan, who shortly after made his appearance.

"Neighbor," said the stranger, "your wife informs me that your cattle are going against you this season."

"She informs you right," said Bryan.

"And why have you not sought a cure?"

"A cure!" re-echoed the man; "why, woman, I have sought cures until I was heartbroken, and all in vain; they get worse every day."

"What will you give me if I cure them for you?"

"Anything in our power," replied Bryan and his wife, both speaking joyfully, and with a breath.

"All I will ask from you is a silver sixpence, and that you will do everything which I will bid you," said she.

The farmer and his wife seemed astonished at the moderation of her demand. They offered her a large sum of money.

"No," said she, "I don't want your money; I am no cheat, and I would not even take sixpence, but that I can do nothing till I handle some of your silver."

The sixpence was immediately given her, and the most implicit obedience promised to her injunctions by both Bryan and his wife, who already began to regard the old beldame as their tutelary angel.

The hag pulled off a black silk ribbon or filet which encircled her head inside her cap, and gave it to Bryan, saying:

"Go, now, and the first cow you touch with this ribbon, turn her into the yard, but be sure you don't touch the second, nor speak a word until you return; be also careful not to let the ribbon touch the ground, for, if you do, all is over."

Bryan took the talismanic ribbon and soon returned, driving a red cow before him.

The old hag went out, and, approaching the cow, commenced pulling hairs out of her tail, at the same time singing some verse in the Irish language, in a low, wild, and unconnected strain. The cow appeared restive and uneasy, but the old witch still continued her mysterious chant until she had the ninth hair extracted. She then ordered the cow to be drove back to her pasture, and again entered the house.

"Go, now," said she to the woman, "and bring me some milk from every cow in your possession."

She went, and soon returned with a large pail filled with a frightful-looking mixture of milk, blood, and corrupt matter. The old woman got it into the churn, and made preparations for churning.

"Now," she said, "you both must churn, make fast the door and windows, and let there be no light but from the fire; do not open your lips until I desire you, and by observing my direction, I make no doubt but, ere the sun goes down, we will find out the infernal villain who is robbing you."

Bryan secured the doors and windows, and commenced churning. The old sorceress sat down by a blazing fire which had been specially lighted for the occasion, and commenced singing the same wild song which she had sung at the pulling of the cow hairs, and after a little time she cast one of the nine hairs into the fire, still singing her mysterious strain, and watching, with intense interest, the witching process.

A loud cry, as if from a female in distress, was now heard approaching the house; the old witch discontinued her incantations, and listened attentively. The crying voice approached the door.

"Open the door quickly," shouted the charmer.

Bryan unbarred the door, and all three rushed out the yard, when they heard the same cry down the *boreheen*, but could see nothing.

"It is all over," shouted the old witch; "something has gone amiss, and our charm for the present is ineffectual."

They now turned back quite crestfallen, when, as they were entering the door, the sybil cast her eyes downward, and perceiving a piece of horseshoe nailed on the threshold, she vociferated:

"Here I have it; no wonder our charm was abortive. The person that was crying abroad is the villain who has your cattle bewitched; I brought her to the house, but she was not able to come to the door on account of that horseshoe. Remove it instantly, and we will try our luck again."

Bryan removed the horseshoe from the doorway, and by the hag's directions placed it on the floor under the churn, having previously reddened it in the fire.

They again resumed their manual operations. Bryan and his wife began to churn, and the witch again to sing her strange verses, and casting her cow hairs into the fire until she had them all nearly exhausted. Her countenance now began to exhibit evident traces of vexation and disappoitment. She got quite pale, her teeth gnashed, her hand trembled, and as she cast the ninth and last hair into the fire, her person exhibited more the appearance of a female demon than of a human being.

Once more the cry was heard, and an aged red-haired woman was seen approaching the house quickly.

"Ho, ho!" roared the sorceress, "I knew it would be so; my charm has succeeded; my expectations are realized, and here she comes, the villain who has destroyed you."

"What are we to do now?" asked Bryan.

"Say nothing to her," said the hag; "give her whatever she demands, and leave the rest to me."

The woman advanced screeching vehemently, and Bryan went out to meet her. She was a neighbor, and she said that one of her best cows was drowning in a pool of water—that there was no one at home but herself, and she implored Bryan to go rescue the cow from destruction.

Bryan accompanied her without hesitation; and having rescued the cow from her perilous situation, was back again in a quarter of an hour.

It was now sunset, and Mrs. Costigan set about preparing supper.

During supper they reverted to the singular transactions of the day. The old witch uttered many a fiendish laugh at the success of her incantations, and inquired who was the woman whom they had so curiously discovered.

Bryan satisfied her in every particular. She was the wife of a neighboring farmer; her name was Rachel Higgins; and she had been long suspected to be on familiar terms with the spirit of darkness. She had five or six cows; but it was observed by her sapient neighbors that she sold more butter every year than other farmers' wives who had twenty. Bryan had, from the commencement of the decline in his cattle, suspected her for being the aggressor, but as he had no proof, he held his peace.

"Well," said the old beldame, with a grim smile, "it is not enough that we have merely discovered the robber; all is in vain if we do not take steps to punish her for the past, as well as to prevent her inroads for the future."

"And how will that be done?" said Bryan.

"I will tell you; as soon as the hour of twelve o'clock arrives tonight, do you go to the pasture, and take a couple of swift-running dogs with you; conceal yourself in some place convenient to the cattle; watch them carefully; and if you see anything, whether man or beast, approach the cows, set on the dogs, and if possible make them draw the blood of the intruder; then *all* will be accomplished. If nothing approaches before sunrise, you may return, and we will try something else."

Convenient there lived the cowherd of a neighboring squire. He was a hardy, courageous young man, and always kept a pair of very ferocious bulldogs. To him Bryan applied for assistance, and he cheerfully agreed to accompany him, and, moreover, proposed to fetch a couple of his master's best grayhounds, as his own dogs, although extremely fierce and bloodthirsty, could not be relied on for swiftness. He promised Bryan to be with him before twelve o'clock, and they parted.

Bryan did not seek sleep that night; he sat up anxiously awaiting the midnight hour. It arrived at last, and his friend, the herdsman, true to his promise, came at the time appointed. After some further admonitions from the *Collough*, they departed. Having arrived at the field, they consulted as to the best position they could choose for concealment. At last they pitched on a small brake of fern, situated at the extremity of the field, adjacent to the boundary ditch, which was thickly studded with large, old white-thorn bushes. Here they crouched themselves, and made the dogs, four in number, lie down beside them, eagerly expecting the appearance of their as yet unknown and mysterious visitor.

Here Bryan and his comrade continued a considerable time in nervous anxiety, still nothing approached, and it became manifest that morning was at hand; they were beginning to grow impatient, and were talking of returning home, when on a sudden they heard a rushing sound behind them, as if proceeding from something endeavoring to force a passage through the thick hedge in their rear. They looked in that direction, and judge of their astonishment, when they perceived a large hare in the act of springing from the ditch, and leaping on the ground quite near them. They were now convinced that this was the object which they had so impatiently expected, and they were resolved to watch her motions narrowly.

After arriving to the ground, she remained motionless for a few moments, looking around her sharply. She then began to skip and jump in a playful manner, now advancing at a smart pace toward the cows and again retreating precipitately, but still drawing nearer and nearer at each sally. At length she advanced up to the next cow, and sucked her for a moment; then on to the next, and so respectively to every cow on the field—the cows all the time lowing loudly, and appearing extremely frightened and agitated. Bryan, from the moment the hare commenced sucking the first, was with difficulty restrained from attacking her; but his more sagacious companion suggested to him that it was better to wait until she would have done, as she would then be much heavier, and more unable to effect her escape than at present. And so the issue proved; for being now done sucking them all, her belly appeared enormously distended, and she made her exit slowly and apparently with difficulty. She advanced toward the hedge where she had entered, and as she arrived just at the clump of ferns where her foes were couched, they started up with a fierce yell, and hallooed the dogs upon her path.

The hare started off at a brisk pace, squirting up the milk she had sucked from her mouth and nostrils, and the dogs making after her rapidly. Rachel Higgins's cabin appeared, through the gray of the morning twilight, at a little distance; and it was evident that puss seemed bent on gaining it, although she made a considerable circuit through the fields in the rear. Bryan and his comrade, however, had their thoughts, and made toward the cabin by the shortest route, and had just arrived as the hare came up panting and almost exhausted, and the dogs at her very scut. She ran round the house, evidently confused and disappointed at the presence of the men, but at length made for the door. In the bottom of the door was a small, semi-circular aperture, resembling those cut in fowl-house doors for the ingress and egress of poultry. To gain this hole, puss now made a last and desperate effort, and had succeeded in forcing her head and shoulders through it, when the foremost of the dogs made a spring and seized her violently by the haunch. She uttered a loud and piercing scream, and struggled desperately to free herself from his grip, and at last succeeded, but not until she left a piece of her rump in his teeth. The men now burst open the door; a bright turf fire blazed on the hearth, and the whole floor was streaming with blood. No hare, however, could be found, and the men were more than ever convinced that it was old Rachel, who had, by the assistance of some demon, assumed the form of the hare, and they now determined to have her if she were over the earth. They entered the bedroom, and heard some smothered groaning, as if proceeding from someone in extreme agony. They went to the corner of the room from whence the moans proceeded, and there, beneath a bundle of freshly-cut rushes, found the form of Rachel Higgins, writhing in the most excruciating agony, and almost smothered in a pool of blood. The men were astounded; they addressed the wretched old woman, but she either could not, or would not, answer them. Her wound still bled copiously; her tortures appeared to increase, and it was evident that she was dying. The aroused family thronged around her with cries and lamentations; she did not seem to heed them, she got worse and worse, and her piercing yells fell awfully on the ears of the bystanders. At length she expired, and her corpse exhibited a most appalling spectacle, even before the spirit had well departed.

Bryan and his friend returned home. The old hag had been previously aware of the fate of Rachel Higgins, but it was not known by what means she acquired her supernatural knowledge. She was delighted at the issue of her mysterious operations. Bryan pressed her much to accept of some remuneration for her services, but she utterly rejected such proposals. She remained a few days at his house, and at length took her leave and departed, no one knew whither.

Old Rachel's remains were interred that night in the neighboring churchyard. Her fate soon became generally known, and her family, ashamed to remain in their native village, disposed of their property, and quitted the country forever. The story, however, is still fresh in the memory of the surrounding villagers; and often, it is said, amid the gray haze of a summer twilight, may the ghost of Rachel Higgins, in the form of a hare, be seen scudding over her favorite and well-remembered haunts.

Donald and His Neighbors
Traditional

HUDDEN AND DUDDEN and Donald O'Nery were near neighbors in the barony of Balinconlig, and plowed with three bullocks; but the two former, envying the present prosperity of the latter, determined to kill his bullock, to prevent his farm from being properly cultivated and labored, that going back in the world he might be induced to sell his lands, which they meant to get possession of. Poor Donald, finding his bullock killed, immediately skinned it, and throwing the skin over his shoulder, with the fleshy side out, set off to the next town with it, to dispose of it to the best of his advantage. Going along the road a magpie flew on the top of the hide, and began picking it, chattering all the time. The bird had been taught to speak, and imitate the human voice, and Donald, thinking he understood some words it was saying, put round his hand and caught hold of it. Having got possession of it, he put it under his greatcoat, and so went on to town. Having sold the hide, he went into an inn to take a dram, and following the landlady into the cellar, he gave the bird a squeeze which made it chatter some broken accents that surprised her very much. "What is that I hear?" said she to Donald. "I think it is talk and yet I do not understand." "Indeed," said Donald, "it is a bird I have that tells me everything, and I always carry it with me to know when there is any danger. "Faith," says he, "it says you have far better liquor than you are giving me." "That is strange," said she, going to another cask of better quality, and asking him if he would sell the bird. "I will," said Donald, "if I get enough for it." "I will fill your hat with silver if you leave it with me." Donald was glad to hear the news, and taking the silver, set off, rejoicing at his good luck. He had not been long at home until he met with Hudden and Dudden. "Mr.," said he, "you thought you had done me a bad turn, but you could not have done me a better; for look here, what I have got for the hide," showing them a hatful of silver; "you never saw such a demand for hides in your life as there is at present." Hudden and Dudden that very night killed their bullocks, and set out the next morning to sell their hides. On coming to the place they went through all the merchants, but could only get a trifle for them; at last they had to take what they could get, and came home in a great rage, and vowing revenge on poor Donald. He had a pretty good guess how matters would turn out, and he being under the kitchen window, he was afraid they would rob him, or perhaps kill him when asleep, and on that account when he was going to bed he left his old mother in his place, and lay down in her bed, which was in the other side of the house, and they taking the old woman for Donald, choked her in her bed, but he making some noise, they had to retreat, and leave the money behind them, which grieved them very much. However by daybreak, Donald got his mother on his back, and carried her to town. Stopping at a well, he fixed his mother with her staff, as if she was stooping for a drink, and then went into a public house convenient and called for a dram. "I wish," said he to a woman that stood near him, "you would tell my mother to come in; she is at yon well trying to get a drink, and she is hard of hearing; if she does not observe you, give her a little shake and tell her that I want her." The woman called her several times, but she seemed to take no notice; at length she went to her and shook her by the arm, but when she let her go again, she tumbled on her head into the well, and, as the woman thought, was drowned. She, in her great surprise and fear at the accident, told Donald what had happened. "O mercy," said he, "what is this?" He ran and pulled her out of the well, weeping and lamenting all the time, and acting in such a manner that you would imagine that he had lost his senses. The woman, on the other hand, was far worse than Donald, for his grief was only feigned, but she imagined herself to be the cause of the old woman's death. The inhabitants of the town, hearing what had happened, agreed to make Donald up a good sum of money for his loss, as the accident happened in their place, and Donald brought a greater sum home with him than he got for the magpie. They buried Donald's mother, and as soon as he saw Hudden and Dudden he showed them the last purse of money he had got. "You thought to kill me last night," said he, "but it was good for me it happened on my mother, for I got all that purse for her to make gunpowder."

That very night Hudden and Dudden killed their mothers, and the next morning set off with them to town. On coming to the town with their burthen on their sacks, they went up and down crying, "Who will buy old wives for gunpowder?" so that everyone laughed at them, and the boys at last clotted them out of the place. They then saw the cheat, and vowed revenge on Donald, buried the old women, and set off in pursuit of him. Coming to his house, they found him sitting at his breakfast, and seizing him, put him in a sack, and went to drown him in a river at some distance. As they were going along the highway they raised a hare, which they saw had but three feet, and throwing off the sack, ran after her, thinking by her appearance she would be easily taken. In their absence there came a drover that way, and hearing Donald singing in the sack, wondered greatly what could be the matter. "What is the reason," said he, "that you are singing, and you confined?" "Oh, I am going to heaven," said Donald, "and in a short time I expect to be free from trouble." "O dear," said the drover, "what will I give you if you let me to your place?" "Indeed, I do not know," said he, "it would take a good sum." "I have not much money," said the drover, "but I have twenty head of fine cattle, which I will give you to exchange places with me." "Well," says Donald, "I do not care if I should loose the sack, and I will come out." In a moment the drover liberated him, and went into the sack himself, and Donald drove home the fine heifers, and left them in his pasture. Hudden and Dudden, having caught the hare, returned, and getting the sack on one of their backs, carried Donald, as they thought, to the river and threw him in, where he immediately sank. They then marched home, intending to take immediate possession of Donald's property, but how great was their surprise when they found him safe at home before them with such a fine herd of cattle, whereas they knew he had none before. "Donald," said they, "what is all this? We thought you were drowned, and yet you are here before us." "Ah !" said he, "if I had but help along with me when you threw me in, it would have been the best job ever I met with, for of all the sight of cattle and gold that ever was seen is there, and no one to own them, but I was not able to manage more than what you see, and I could show you the spot where you might get hundreds." They both swore they would be his friend, and Donald accordingly led them to a very deep part of the river, and lifted up a stone. "Now," said he, "Watch this," throwing it into the stream; "there is the very place, and go in, one of you first, and if you want help, you have nothing to do but call." Hudden jumping in, and sinking to the bottom, rose up again, and making a bubbling noise, as those do that are drowning, attempted to speak, but could not. "What is that he is saying now?" says Dudden "Faith," says Donald, "he is calling for help; don't you hear him?" "Stand about," said he, running back, "till I leap in. I know how to do it better than any of you." Dudden, to have the advantage of him, jumped in off the bank, and was drowned along with Hudden, and this was the end of Hudden and Dudden.

A Play-House in the Waste
George Moore

"IT'S A CLOSED MOUTH that can hold a good story," as the saying goes, and very soon it got about that Father MacTurnan had written to Rome saying he was willing to take a wife to his bosom for patriotic reasons, if the Pope would relieve him of his vow of celibacy. And many phrases and words from his letter (translated by whom—by the Bishop or Father Meehan?— nobody ever knew) were related over the Dublin firesides, till at last out of the talk a tall gaunt man emerged, in an old overcoat, green from weather and wear, the tails of it flapping as he rode his bicycle through the great waste bog that lies between Belmullet and Crossmolina. His name! We liked it. It appealed to our imagination. MacTurnan! It conveyed something from afar like Hamlet or Don Quixote. He seemed as near and as far from us as they, till Pat Comer, one of the organizers of the

IAOS, came in and said, after listening to the talk that was going round:

"Is it of the priest that rides in the great Mayo bog you are speaking? If it is, you haven't got the story rightly." As he told us the story, so it is printed in this book. And we sat wondering greatly, for we seemed to see a soul on its way to heaven. But round a fire there is always one who cannot get off the subject of women and blasphemy—a papist generally he is; and it was Quinn that evening who kept plaguing us with jokes, whether it would be a fat girl or a thin that the priest would choose if the Pope gave him leave to marry, until at last, losing all patience with him, I bade him be silent, and asked Pat Comer to tell us if the priest was meditating a new plan for Ireland's salvation. "For a mind like his," I said, "would not stand still and problems such as ours waiting to be solved."

"You're wrong there! He thinks no more of Ireland, and neither reads nor plans, but knits stockings ever since the wind took his play-house away."

"Took his play-house away!" said several.

"And why would he be building a play-house," somebody asked, "and he living in a waste?"

"A queer idea, surely!" said another. "A play-house in the waste!"

"Yes, a queer idea," said Pat, "but a true one all the same, for I have seen it with my own eyes—or the ruins of it—and not later back than three weeks ago, when I was staying with the priest himself. You know the road, all of you—how it straggles from Foxford through the bog alongside of bogholes deep enough to drown one, and into which the jarvey and myself seemed in great likelihood of pitching, for the car went down into great ruts, and the horse was shying from one side of the road to the other, and at nothing so far as we could see."

"There's nothing to be afeared of, yer honor; only once was he near leaving the road, the day before Christmas, and I driving the doctor. It was here he saw it—a white thing gliding—and the wheel of the car must have gone within an inch of the boghole."

"And the doctor. Did he see it?" I said.

"He saw it too, and so scared was he that the hair rose up and went through his cap."

"Did the jarvey laugh when he said that?" we asked Pat Comer; and Pat answered: "Not he! Them fellows just speak as the words come to them without thinking. Let me get on with my story. We drove on for about a mile, and it was to stop him from clicking his tongue at the horse that I asked him if the bog was Father MacTurnan's parish." "Every mile of it, sir," he said, "every mile of it, and we do be seeing him buttoned up in his old coat riding along the roads on his bicycle going to sick calls."

"Do you often be coming this road?" says I.

"Not very often, sir. No one lives here except the poor people, and the priest and the doctor. Faith! there isn't a poorer parish in Ireland, and every one of them would have been dead long ago if it had not been for Father James."

"And how does he help them?"

"Isn't he always writing letters to the Government asking for relief works? Do you see those bits of roads?"

"Where do those roads lead to?"

"Nowhere. Them roads stops in the middle of the bog when the money is out."

"But," I said, "surely it would be better if the money were spent upon permanent improvements—on drainage, for instance."

The jarvey didn't answer; he called to his horse, and not being able to stand the clicking of his tongue, I kept on about the drainage.

"There's no fall, sir."

"And the bog is too big," I added, in hope of encouraging conversation.

"Faith it is, sir."

"But we aren't very far from the sea, are we?"

"About a couple of miles."

"Well then," I said, "couldn't a harbor be made?"

"They were thinking about that, but there's no depth of water, and everyone's against emigration now."

"Ah! the harbor would encourage emigration."

"So it would, your honor."

"But is there no talk about home industries, weaving, lacemaking?"

"I won't say that."

"But has it been tried?"

"The candle do be burning in the priest's window till one in the morning, and he sitting up thinking of plans to keep the people at home. Now, do ye see that house, sir, fornint my whip at the top of the hill? Well, that's the play-house he built."

"A play-house?"

"Yes, yer honor. Father James hoped the people might come from Dublin to see it, for no play like it had ever been acted in Ireland before, sir!"

"And was the play performed?"

"No, yer honor. The priest had been learning them all the summer, but the autumn was on them before they had got it by rote, and a wind came and blew down one of the walls."

"And couldn't Father MacTurnan get the money to build it up?"

"Sure, he might have got the money, but where'd be the use

when there was no luck in it?"

"And who were to act the play?"

"The girls and the boys in the parish, and the prettiest girl in all the parish was to play Good Deeds."

"So it was a miracle play," I said.

"Do you see that man? It's the priest coming out of Tom Burke's cabin, and I warrant he do be bringing him the Sacrament, and he having the holy oils with him, for Tom won't pass the day; we had the worst news of him last night."

"And I can tell you," said Pat Comer, dropping his story for a moment and looking round the circle, "it was a sad story the jarvey told me. He told it well, for I can see the one-roomed hovel full of peatsmoke, the black iron pot with traces of the yellow stirabout in it on the hearth, and the sick man on the pallet bed, and the priest by his side mumbling prayers together. Faith! these jarveys can tell a story–none better."

"As well as yourself, Pat," one of us said. And Pat began to tell of the miles of bog on either side of the straggling road, of the hill-top to the left, with the play-house showing against the dark and changing clouds; of a woman in a red petticoat, a handkerchief tied round her head, who had flung down her spade the moment she caught sight of the car, of the man who appeared on the brow and blew a horn. "For she mistook us for bailiffs," said Pat, "and two little sheep hardly bigger than geese were driven away."

"A play-house in the waste for these people," I was saying to myself all the time, till my meditations were interrupted by the jarvey telling that the rocky river we crossed was called the Greyhound—a not inappropriate name, for it ran swiftly . . . Away down the long road a white cottage appeared, and the jarvey said to me, "That is the priest's house." It stood on the hillside some little way from the road, and all the way to the door I wondered how his days passed in the great loneliness of the bog.

"His reverence isn't at home, yer honor—he's gone to attend a sick call."

"Yes, I know—Tom Burke."

"And is Tom better, Mike?"

"The devil a bether he'll be this side of Jordan," the jarvey answered, and the housekeeper showed me into the priest's parlor. It was lined with books, and I looked forward to a pleasant chat when we had finished our business. At that time I was on a relief committee, and the people were starving in the poor parts of the country.

"I think he'll be back in about an hour's time, yer honor." But the priest seemed to be detained longer than his housekeeper expected, and the moaning of the wind round the cottage reminded me of the small white thing the horse and the doctor had seen gliding along the road. "The priest knows the story—he will tell me," I said, and piled more turf on the fire—fine sods of hard black turf they were, and well do I remember seeing them melting away. But all of a sudden my eyes closed. I couldn't have been asleep more than a few minutes when it seemed to me a great crowd of men and women had gathered about the house, and a moment after the door was flung open, and a tall, gaunt man faced me.

"I've just come," he said, "from a deathbed, and they that have followed me aren't far from death if we don't succeed in getting help." I don't know how I can tell you of the crowd I saw round the house that day. We are accustomed to see poor people in towns cowering under arches, but it is more pitiful to see people starving in the fields on the mountain side. I don't know why it should be so, but it is. But I call to mind two men in ragged trousers and shirts as ragged, with brown beards on faces yellow with famine; and the words of one of them are not easily forgotten: "The white sun of Heaven doesn't shine upon two poorer men than upon this man and myself." I can tell you I didn't envy the priest his job, living all his life in the waste listening to tales of starvation, looking into famished faces. There were some women among them, kept back by the men, who wanted to get their word in first. They seemed to like to talk about their misery . . . and I said:

"They are tired of seeing each other. I am a spectacle, a show, an amusement for them. I don't know if you can catch my meaning?"

"I think I do," Father James answered. And I asked him to come for a walk up the hill and show me the play-house.

Again he hesitated, and I said: "You must come, Father MacTurnan, for a walk. You must forget the misfortunes of those people for a while." He yielded, and we spoke of the excellence of the road under our feet, and he told me that when he conceived the idea of a play-house, he had already succeeded in persuading the inspector to agree that the road they were making should go to the top of the hill. "The policy of the Government," he said, "from the first was that relief works should benefit nobody except the workers, and it is sometimes very difflcult to think out a project for work that will be perfectly useless. Arches have been built on the top of hills, and roads that lead nowhere. A strange sight to the stranger a road must be that stops suddenly in the middle of a bog. One wonders at first how a Government could be so foolish, but when one thinks of it, it is easy to understand that the Government doesn't wish to spend money on works that will benefit a class. But the road that leads nowhere is difficult to make, even though starving men are employed upon it; for a man to work well there must be an end in view, and I can tell you it is difficult to bring even starving men to engage on a road that leads nowhere. If I'd told everything I am telling you to the inspector, he wouldn't have agreed to let the road run to the top of the hill; but I said to him: "The road leads nowhere; as well let it end at the top of the hill as down in the valley." So I got the money for my road and some money for my play-house, for of course the play-house was as useless as the road; a play-house in the waste can neither interest or benefit anybody! But there was an idea at the back of my mind all the time that when the road and the play-house were finished, I might be able to induce the Government to build a harbor?"

"But the harbor would be of use."

"Of very little," he answered. "For the harbor to be of use a great deal of dredging would have to be done."

"And the Government needn't undertake the dredging. How very ingenious! I suppose you often come here to read your breviary?"

"During the building of the play-house I often used to be up here, and during the rehearsals I was here every day."

"If there was a rehearsal," I said to myself, "there must have been a play." And I affected interest in the grey shallow sea and the erosion of the low-lying land—a salt marsh filled with pools.

"I thought once," said the priest, "that if the play were a great success, a line of flat-bottomed steamers might be built."

"Sitting here in the quiet evenings," I said to myself, "reading his breviary, dreaming of a line of steamships crowded with visitors! He has been reading about the Oberammergau performances." So that was his game—the road, the playhouse, the harbor—and I agreed with him that no one would have dared to predict that visitors would have come from all sides of Europe to see a few peasants performing a miracle play in the

Tyrol.

"Come," I said, "into the play-house and let me see how you built it."

Half a wall and some of the roof had fallen, and the rubble had not been cleared away, and I said:

"It will cost many pounds to repair the damage, but having gone so far you should give the play a chance."

"I don't think it would be advisable," he muttered, half to himself, half to me.

As you may well imagine, I was anxious to hear if he had discovered any aptitude for acting among the girls and the boys who lived in the cabins.

"I think," he answered me, "that the play would have been fairly acted; I think that, with a little practice, we might have done as well as they did at Oberammergau."

An odd man, more willing to discuss the play that he had chosen than the talents of those who were going to perform it, and he told me that it had been written in the fourteenth century in Latin, and that he had translated it into Irish.

I asked him if it would have been possible to organize an excursion from Dublin—"Oberammergau in the West."

"I used to think so. But it is eight miles from Rathowen, and the road is a bad one, and when they got here there would be no place for them to stay; they would have to go all the way back again, and that would be sixteen miles."

"Yet you did well, Father James, to build the play-house, for the people could work better while they thought they were accomplishing something. Let me start a subscription for you in Dublin."

"I don't think that it would be possible—"

"Not for me to get fifty pounds?"

"You might get the money, but I don't think we could ever get a performance of the play."

"And why not?" I said.

"You see, the wind came and blew down the wall. The people are very pious; I think they felt that the time they spent rehearsing might have been better spent. The play-house disturbed them in their ideas. They hear Mass on Sundays, and there are the Sacraments, and they remember they have to die. It used to seem to me a very sad thing to see all the people going to America; the poor Celt disappearing in America, leaving his own country, leaving his language, and very often his religion."

"And does it no longer seem to you sad that such a thing should happen?"

"No, not if it is the will of God. God has specially chosen the Irish race to convert the world. No race has provided so many missionaries, no race has preached the Gospel more frequently to the heathen; and once we realize that we have to die, and very soon, and that the Catholic Church is the only true Church, our ideas about race and nationality fade from us. We are here, not to make life successful and triumphant, but to gain heaven. That is the truth, and it is to the honor of the Irish people that they have been selected by God to preach the truth, even though they lose their nationality in preaching it. I do not expect you to accept these opinions. I know that you think very differently, but living here I have learned to acquiesce in the will of God."

He stopped speaking suddenly, like one ashamed of having expressed himself too openly, and soon after we were met by a number of peasants, and the priest's attention was engaged; the inspector of the relief works had to speak to him; and I didn't see him again until dinner-time.

"You have given them hope," he said.

This was gratifying to hear, and the priest sat listening while I told him of the looms already established in different parts of the country. We talked about half an hour, and then, like one who suddenly remembers, the priest got up and fetched his knitting.

"Do you knit every evening?"

"I have got into the way of knitting lately—it passes the time."

"But do you never read?" I asked, and my eyes went towards the bookshelves.

"I used to read a great deal. But there wasn't a woman in the parish that could turn a heel properly, so I had to learn to knit."

"Do you like knitting better than reading?" I asked, feeling ashamed of my curiosity.

"I have constantly to attend sick calls, and if one is absorbed in a book one doesn't like to put it aside."

"I see you have two volumes of miracle plays!"

"Yes, and that's another danger: a book begets all kinds of ideas and notions into one's head. The idea of that play-house came out of those books."

"But," I said, "you don't think that God sent the storm because He didn't wish a play to be performed?"

"One cannot judge God's designs. Whether God sent the storm or whether it was accident must remain a matter for conjecture; but it is not a matter of conjecture that one is doing certain good by devoting oneself to one's daily task, getting the Government to start new relief works, establishing schools for weaving. The people are entirely dependent upon me, and when I'm attending to their wants I know I'm doing right."

The play-house interested me more than the priest's ideas of right and wrong, and I tried to get him back to it; but the subject seemed a painful one, and I said to myself: "The jarvey will tell me all about it tomorrow. I can rely on him to find out the whole story from the housekeeper in the kitchen." And sure enough, we hadn't got to the Greyhound River before he was leaning across the well of the car talking to me and asking if the priest was thinking of putting up the wall of the play-house.

"The wall of the play-house?" I said.

"Yes, yer honor. Didn't I see both of you going up the hill in the evening time?"

"I don't think we shall ever see a play in the play-house."

"Why would we, since it was God that sent the wind that blew it down?"

"How do you know it was God that sent the wind? It might have been the devil himself, or somebody's curse."

"Sure it is of Mrs. Sheridan you do be thinking, yer honor, and of her daughter—she that was to be playing Good Deeds in the play, yer honor; and wasn't she wake coming home from the learning of the play? And when the signs of her wakeness began to show, the widow Sheridan took a halter off the cow and tied Margaret to the wall, and she was in the stable till the child was born. Then didn't her mother take a bit of string and tie it round the child's throat, and bury it near the play-house; and it was three nights after that the storm rose, and the child pulled the thatch out of the roof."

"But did she murder the child?"

"Sorra wan of me knows. She sent for the priest when she was dying, and told him what she had done."

"But the priest wouldn't tell what he heard in the confessional," I said.

"Mrs. Sheridan didn't die that night; not till the end of the week, and the neighbors heard her talking of the child she had buried, and then they all knew what the white thing was they had seen by the roadside. The night the priest left her he saw the white thing standing in front of him, and if he hadn't been a priest he'd have dropped down dead; so he took some water from the boghole and dashed it over it, saying, 'I baptise thee in the name of the Father, and of the Son, and of the Holy Ghost!'"

The driver told his story like one saying his prayers, and he seemed to have forgotten that he had a listener.

"It must have been a great shock to the priest."

"Faith it was, sir, to meet an unbaptised child on the roadside, and that child the only bastard that was ever born in the parish—so Tom Mulhare says, and he's the oldest man in the county."

"It was altogether a very queer idea—this play-house."

"It was indeed, sir, a quare idea, but you see he's a quare man. He has been always thinking of something to do good, and it is said that he thinks too much. Father James is a very quare man, your honor."

The Legend of Knockgrafton
Thomas Crofton Crocker

THERE WAS ONCE a poor man who lived in the fertile glen of Aherlow, at the foot of the gloomy Galtee mountains, and he had a great hump on his back: he looked just as if his body had been rolled up and placed upon his shoulders; and his head was pressed down with the weight so much that his chin, when he was sitting, used to rest upon his knees for support. The country people were rather shy of meeting him in any lonesome place, for though, poor creature, he was as harmless and as inoffensive as a new-born infant, yet his deformity was so great that he scarcely appeared to be a human creature, and some ill-minded persons had set strange stories about him afloat. He was said to have a great knowledge of herbs and charms; but certain it was that he had a mighty skilful hand in plaiting straws and rushes into hats and baskets, which was the way he made his livelihood.

Lusmore, for that was the nickname put upon him by reason of his always wearing a sprig of the fairy cap, or lusmore (the foxglove), in his little straw hat, would ever get a higher penny for his plaited work than anyone else, and perhaps that was the reason why someone, out of envy, had circulated the strange stories about him. Be that as it may, it happened that he was returning one evening from the pretty town of Cahir toward Cappagh, and as little Lusmore walked very slowly, on account of the great hump upon his back, it was quite dark when he came to the old moat of Knockgrafton, which stood on the right-hand side of his road.

Tired and weary was he, and noways comfortable in his own mind at thinking how much farther he had to travel, and that he should be walking all the night; so he sat down under the moat to rest himself, and began looking mournfully enough upon the moon, which

"Rising in clouded majesty, at length
Apparent Queen, unveil'd her peerless light,
And o'er the dark her silver mantle threw."

Presently there rose a wild strain of unearthly melody upon the ear of little Lusmore; he listened, and he thought that he had never heard such ravishing music before. It was like the sound of many voices, each mingling and blending with the other so strangely that they seemed to be one, though all singing different strains, and the words of the song were these:

Da Luan, Da Mort, Da Luan, Da Mort, Da Luan, Da Mort;

There would be a moment's pause, and then the round of melody went on again.

Lusmore listened attentively, scarcely drawing his breath lest he might lose the slightest note. He now plainly perceived that the singing was within the moat; and though at first it had charmed him so much, he began to get tired of hearing the same round sung over and over so often without any change; so availing himself of the pause when *Da Luan, Da Mort*, had been sung three times, he took up the tune, and raised it with the words *agus Da Dardeen,* and then went on singing with the voices inside of the moat, *Da Luan, Da Mort,* finishing the melody, when the pause again came, with *agus Da Dardeen.**

The fairies within Knockgrafton, for the song was a fairy melody, when they heard this addition to the tune, were so much delighted that, with instant resolve, it was determined to bring the mortal among them, whose musical skill so far exceeded theirs, and little Lusmore was conveyed into their company with the eddying speed of a whirlwind.

Glorious to behold was the sight that burst upon him as he came down through the moat, twirling round and round, with the lightness of a straw, to the sweetest music that kept time to his motion. The greatest honor was then paid him, for he was put above all the musicians, and he had servants tending upon him, and everything to his heart's content, and a hearty welcome to all; and, in short, he was made as much of as if he had been the first man in the land.

Presently Lusmore saw a great consultation going forward among the fairies, and, notwithstanding all their civility, he felt very much frightened, until one stepping out from the rest came up to him and said:

"Lusmore! Lusmore!

---

* The words *La Luan, Da Mort agus Da Dardeen* are Irish for "Monday, Tuesday, and Wednesday too."

Doubt not, nor deplore,
For the hump which you bore
On your back is no more;
Look down on the floor,
And view it, Lusmore! Lusmore!"

When these words were said poor little Lusmore felt himself so light, and so happy, that he thought he could have bounded at one jump over the moon, like the cow in the history of the cat and the fiddle; and he saw, with inexpressible pleasure, his hump tumble down upon the ground from his shoulders. He then tried to lift up his head, and he did so with becoming caution, fearing that he might knock it against the ceiling of the grand hall, where he was; he looked round and round again with the greatest wonder and delight upon everything, which appeared more and more beautiful; and, overpowered at beholding such a resplendent scene, his head grew dizzy, and his eyesight became dim. At last he fell into a sound sleep, and when he awoke he found that it was broad daylight, the sun shining brightly, and the birds singing sweetly; and that he was lying just at the foot of the moat of Knockgrafton, with the cows and sheep grazing peacefully round about him. The first thing Lusmore did, after saying his prayers, was to put his hand behind to feel for his hump, but no sign of one was there on his back, and he looked at himself with great pride, for he had now become a well-shaped, dapper little fellow, and more than that, found himself in a full suit of new clothes, which he concluded the fairies had made for him.

Toward Cappagh he went, stepping out as lightly, and springing up at every step as if he had been all his life dancing-master. Not a creature who met Lusmore knew him without his hump, and he had a great work to persuade everyone that he was the same man—in truth he was not, so far as the outward

THE LEGEND OF KNOCKGRAFTON

appearances went.

Of course it was not long before the story of Lusmore's hump got about, and a great wonder was made of it. Through the country, for miles round, it was the talk of everyone, high and low.

One morning, as Lusmore was sitting contented enough at his cabin door, up came an old woman to him and asked him if he could direct her to Cappagh.

"I need give you no directions, my good woman," said Lusmore, "for this is Cappagh; and whom may you want here?"

"I have come," said the woman, "out of Decie's country, in the county of Waterford, looking after one Lusmore, who, I have heard tell, had his hump taken off by the fairies; for there is a son of a gossip of mine who has got a hump on him that will be his death; and maybe, if he could use the same charm as Lusmore the hump may be taken off him. And now I have told you the reason of my coming so far: 'tis to find out about this charm, if I can."

Lusmore, who was ever a good-natured little fellow, told the woman all the particulars, how he had raised the tune for the fairies at Knockgrafton, how his hump had been removed from his shoulders, and how he had got a new suit of clothes into the bargain.

The woman thanked him very much, and then went away quite happy and easy in her own mind. When she came back to her gossip's house, in the county of Waterford, she told her everything that Lusmore had said and they put the little hump-backed man, who was a peevish and cunning creature from his birth, upon a car, and took him all the way across the county. It was a long journey, but they did not care for that, so the hump was taken from off him; and they brought him, just at nightfall, and left him under the old moat of Knockgrafton.

Jack Madden, for that was the humpy man's name, had not been sitting there long when he heard the tune going on within the moat much sweeter than before; for the fairies were singing it the way Lusmore had settled their music for them, and the song was going on: *Da Luan, Da Mort, Da Luan, Da Mort, Da Luan, Da Mort, agus Da Dardeen,* without ever stopping. Jack Madden, who was in a great hurry to get quit of his hump, never thought of waiting until the fairies had done, or watching for a fit opportunity to raise the tune higher again than Lusmore had; so having heard them sing it over seven times without stopping, out he bawls, never minding the time or the humor of the tune, or how he could bring his words in properly, *agus Da Dardeen, agus Da Hena,* thinking that if one day was good, two were better; and that if Lusmore had one new suit of clothes given him, he should have two.*

No sooner had the words passed his lips than he was taken up and whisked into the moat with prodigious force; and the fairies came crowding round about him with great anger, screeching and screaming, and roaring out:

"Who spoiled our tune? Who spoiled our tune?" and one stepped up to him above all the rest, and said:

"Jack Madden, Jack Madden
Your words come so bad in
The tune we felt glad in;—
This castle you're had in,
That your life we may sadden;
Here's two humps for Jack Madden!"

And twenty of the strongest fairies brought Lusmore's hump, and put it down upon poor Jack's back, over his own, where it became fixed as firmly as if it was nailed on with twelve-penny

---

* *Da Hena* is Thursday.

nails, by the best carpenter that ever drove one. Out of their castle they then kicked him; and in the morning, when Jack Madden's mother and her gossip came to look after their little man, they found him half dead, lying at the foot of the moat, with the other hump upon his back. Well to be sure, how they did look at each other! but they were afraid to say anything, lest a hump might be put upon their own shoulders. Home they brought the unlucky Jack Madden with them, as downcast in their hearts and their looks as ever two gossips were; and what through the weight of his other hump, and the long journey, he died soon after, leaving, they say, his heavy curse to anyone who would go to listen to fairy tunes again.

The Crucifixion of the Outcast
W. B. Yeats

A MAN, with thin brown hair and a pale face, half ran, half walked, along the road that wound from the south to the town of Sligo. Many called him Cumhal, the son of Cormac, and many called him the Swift Wild Horse; and he was a gleeman, and he wore a short particolored doublet, and had pointed shoes, with a bulging wallet. Also he was of the blood of the Ernaans, and his birthplace was the Field of Gold; but his eating and sleeping places were in the five kingdoms of Eri, and his abiding place was not upon the ridge of the earth. His eyes strayed from the tower of what was later the Abbey of the White Friars to a row of crosses which stood out against the sky upon a hill a little to the eastward of the town, and he clenched his fist, and shook it at the crosses. He knew they were not empty, for the birds were fluttering about them; and he thought how, as like it as not, just such another vagabond as himself had been mounted on one of them; and he muttered: "If it were hanging or bow-stringing, or stoning or beheading, it would be bad enough. But to have the birds pecking your eyes and the wolves eating your feet! I would that the red wind of the Druids had withered in his cradle the soldier of Dathi, who brought the tree of death out of barbarous lands, or that the lightning, when it smote Dathi at the foot of the mountain, had smitten him also, or that his grave had been dug by the green-haired and green-toothed merrows deep at the roots of the deep sea."

While he spoke, he shivered from head to foot, and the sweat came out upon his face, and he knew not why, for he had looked upon many crosses. He passed over two hills and under the battlemented gate, and then round by a left-hand way to the door of the Abbey. It was studded with great nails, and when he knocked at it he roused the lay brother who was the porter, and of him he asked a place in the guest-house. Then the lay brother took a glowing turf on a shovel, and led the way to a big and naked outhouse strewn with very dirty rushes; and lighted a rush-candle fixed between two of the stones of the wall, and set the glowing turf upon the hearth and gave him two unlighted sods and a wisp of straw, and showed him a blanket hanging from a nail, and a shelf with a loaf of bread and a jug of water, and a tub in a far corner. Then the lay brother left him and went back to his place by the door. And Cumhal the son of Cormac began to blow upon the glowing turf that he might light the two sods and the wisp of straw; but the sods and the straw would not light, for they were damp. So he took off his pointed shoes, and drew the tub out of the corner with the thought of washing the dust of the highway from his feet; but the water was so dirty that he could not see the bottom. He was very hungry, for he had not eaten all that day, so he did not waste much anger upon the tub, but took up the black loaf, and bit into it, and then spat out the bite, for the bread was hard and mouldy. Still he did not give way to his anger, for he had not drunken these many hours; having a hop of heath beer or wine at his day's end, he had left the brooks untasted, to make his supper the more delightful. Now he put the jug to his lips, but he flung it from him straightway, for the water was bitter and ill-smelling. Then he gave the jug a kick, so that it broke against the opposite wall, and he took down the blanket to wrap it about him for the night. But no sooner did he touch it than it was alive with skipping fleas. At this, beside himself with anger, he rushed to the door of the guest-house, but the lay brother, being well accustomed to such outcries, had locked it on the outside; so he emptied the tub and began to beat the door with it, till the lay brother came to the door and asked what ailed him, and why he woke him out of sleep. "What ails me!" shouted Cumhal; "are not the sods as wet as the sands of the Three Rosses? and are not the fleas in the blanket as many as the waves of the sea and as lively? and is not the bread as hard as the heart of a lay brother who has forgotten God? and is not the water in the jug as bitter and as ill-smelling as his soul? and is not the foot-water the color that shall be upon him when he has been charred in the Undying Fires?" The lay brother saw that the lock was fast, and went back to his niche, for he was too sleepy to talk with comfort. And Cumhal went on beating at the door, and presently he heard the lay brother's foot once more, and cried out at him. "O cowardly and tyrannous race of monks, persecutors of the bard and the gleeman, haters of life and joy! O race that does not draw the sword and tell the truth! O race that melts the bones of the people with cowardice and with deceit!"

"Gleeman," said the lay brother, "I also makes rhymes; I make many while I sit in my niche by the door, and I sorrow to hear the bards railing upon the monks. Brother, I would sleep, and therefore I make known to you that it is the head of the monastery, our gracious abbot, who orders all things concerning the lodging of travelers."

"You may sleep," said Cumhal, "I will sing a bard's curse on the abbot." And he set the tub upside down under the window, and stood upon it, and began to sing in a very loud voice. The singing awoke the abbot, so that he sat up in bed and blew a silver whistle until the lay brother came to him. "I cannot get a wink of deep with that noise," said the abbot. What is happening?"

"It is a gleeman," said the lay brother, "who complains of the sods, of the bread. of the water in the jug, of the foot-water, and of the blanket. And now he is singing a bard's curse upon you, O brother abbot, and upon your father and your mother, and your grandfather and your grandmother, and upon all your relations."

"Is he cursing in rhyme?"

"He is cursing in rhyme, and with two assonances in every line of his curse."

The abbot pulled his nightcap off and crumpled it in his hands, and the circular grey patch of hair in the middle of his bald head looked like the cairn upon Knocknarea, for in Connaught they had not yet abandoned the ancient tonsure. "Unless we do somewhat," he said, "he will teach his curses to the children in the street, and the girls spinning at the doors, and to the robbers upon Ben Bulben."

"Shall I go, then," said the other, "and give him dry sods, a fresh loaf, clean water in a jug, clean foot-water, and a new blanket, and make him swear by the blessed Saint Benignus, and by the sun and moon, that no bond be lacking, not to tell his rhymes to the children in the street, and the girls spinning at the doors, and the robbers upon Ben Bulben?"

"Neither our Blessed Patron nor the sun and moon would avail at all," said the abbot; "for tomorrow or the next day the mood to curse would come upon him, or a pride in those rhymes would move him, and he would teach his lines to the children, and the girls, and the robbers. Or else he would tell another of his craft how he fared in the guest-house, and he in his turn would begin to curse, and my name would wither. For learn there is no steadfastness of purpose upon the roads, but only under roofs and between four walls. Therefore I bid you go and awaken Brother Kevin, Brother Dove, Brother Little Wolf, Brother Bald Patrick, Brother Bald Brandon, Brother James, and Brother Peter. And they shall take the man, and bind him with ropes, and dip him in the river that he shall cease to sing. And in the morning, lest this but make him curse the louder, we will crucify him."

"The crosses are all full," said the lay brother.

"Then we must make another cross. If we do not make an end to him another will, for who can eat and sleep in peace while men like him are going about the world? We would stand shamed indeed before blessed Saint Benignus, and sour would be his face when he comes to judge us at the Last Day, were we to spare an enemy of his when we had him under our thumb! Brother, there is not one of these bards and gleemen who has not scattered his bastards through the five kingdoms, and if they slit a purse or a throat, and it is always one or the other, it never comes into their heads to confess and do penance. Can you name one that is not heathen at heart, always longing after the Son of Lir, and Aengus, and Bridget, and the Dagda, and Dana the Mother, and all the false gods of the old days; always making poems in praise of those kings and queens of the demons, Finvaragh, whose home is under Cruachmaa, and Red Aodh of Cnocna-Sidhe, and Cleena of the Wave, and Aoibhell of the Grey Rock, and him they call Donn of the Vats of the Sea; and railing against God and Christ and the blessed Saints." While he was speaking he crossed himself, and when he had finished he drew the nightcap over his ears to shut out the noise, and closed his eyes and composed himself to sleep.

The lay brother found Brother Kevin, Brother Dove, Brother Little Wolf, Brother Bald Patrick, Brother Bald Brandon, Brother James, and Brother Peter sitting up in bed, and he made them get up. Then they bound Cumhal, and they dragged him to the river, and they dipped him in it at the place which was afterwards called Buckley's Ford.

"Gleeman," said the lay brother, as they led him back to the guest-house, "why do you ever use the wit which God has given you to make blasphemous and immoral tales and verses? For such is the way of your craft. I have, indeed. many such tales and verses well-nigh by rote, and so I know that I speak true! And why do you praise with rhyme those demons, Finvaragh, Red Aodh, Cleena, Aoibhell and Donn? I, too, am a man of great wit and learning, but I ever glorify our gracious abbot, and Benignus our Patron, and the princes of the province. My soul is decent and orderly, but yours is like the wind among the salley gardens. I said what I could for you, being also a man of many thoughts, but who could help such a one as you?"

"Friend," answered the gleeman, "my soul is indeed like the wind, and it blows me to and fro, and up and down, and puts many things into my mind and out of my mind, and therefore am I called the Swift Wild Horse." And he spoke no more that night, for his teeth were chattering with the cold.

The abbot and the monks came to him in the morning, and

bade him get ready to be crucified, and led him out of the guesthouse. And while he still stood upon the step, a flock of great grass-barnacles passed high above him with clanking cries. He lifted his arms to them and said, "O great grass-barnacles, tarry a little, and mayhap my soul will tread with you to the waste places of the shore and to the ungovernable sea!" At the gate a crowd of beggars gathered about them. being come there to beg from any traveler or pilgrim who might have spent the night in the guest-house. The abbot and the monks led the gleeman to a place in the woods at some distance, where many straight young trees were growing, and they made him cut one down and fashion it to the right length, while the beggars stood round them in a ring, talking and gesticulating. The abbot then bade him cut off another and shorter piece of wood, and nail it upon the first. So there was his cross for him, and they put it upon his shoulder, for his crucifixion was to be on the top of the hill where the others were. A half-mile on the way he asked them to stop and see him juggle for them; for he knew, he said, all the tricks of Aengus the Sublehearted. The old monks were for pressing on, but the young monks would see him: so he did many wonders for them, even to the drawing of live frogs out of his ears. But after a while he turned on him, and said his tricks were dull and a little unholy, and set the cross on his shoulders again. Another half-mile on the way and he asked them to stop and hear him jest for them, for he knew, he said, all the jests of Conan the Bald, upon whose back a sheep's wool grew. And the young monks, when they had heard his merry tales, again bade him take up his cross, for it ill became them to listen to such follies. Another half-mile on the way, he asked them to stop and hear him sing the story of White-breasted Deirdre, and how she endured many sorrows, and how the sons of Usna died to serve her. And the young monks were mad to hear him, but when he had ended they grew angry, and beat him for waking forgotten longings in their hearts. So they set the cross upon his back and hurried him to the hill.

When he was come to the top, they took the cross from him, and began to dig a hole for it to stand in, while the beggars gathered round, and talked among themselves. "I ask a favor before I die," says Cumhal.

"We will grant you no more delays," says the abbot.

"I ask no more delays, for I have drawn the sword, and told the truth, and lived my dream. and am content."

"Would you, then, confess?"

"By sun and moon, not I; I ask but to be let eat the food I carry in my wallet. I carry food in my wallet whenever I go upon a journey, but I do not taste of it unless I am well-nigh starved. I have not eaten now these two days."

"You may eat, then," says the abbot, and he turned to help the monks dig the hole.

The gleeman took a loaf and some strips of cold fried bacon out of his wallet and laid them upon the ground. "I will give a tithe to the poor," says he, and he cut a tenth part from the loaf and the bacon. "Who among you is the poorest?" And thereupon was a great clamor, for the beggars began the history of their sorrows and their poverty, and their yellow faces swayed like Gara Lough when the floods have filled it with water from the bogs.

He listened for a little, and, says he, "I am myself the poorest, for I have traveled the bare road, and by the edges of the sea; and the tattered doublet of particolored cloth upon my back and the torn pointed shoes upon my feet have ever irked me, because of the towered city full of noble raiment which was in my heart. And I have been the more alone upon the roads and by the sea because I heard in my heart the rustling of the rose-bordered dress of her who is more subtle than Aengus the Subtlehearted, and more full of the beauty of laughter than Conan the Bald, and more full of wisdom of tears than White-breasted Deirdre, and more lovely than a bursting dawn to them that are lost in the darkness. Therefore, I award the tithe to myself; but yet, because I am done with all things, I give it unto you."

So he flung the bread and the strips of bacon among the beggars, and they fought with many cries until the last scrap was eaten. But meanwhile the monks nailed the gleeman to his cross, and set it upright in the hole, and shoveled the earth into the hole and trampled it level and hard. So then they went away, but the beggars stayed on, sitting round the cross. But when the sun was sinking, they also got up to go, for the air was getting chilly. And as soon as they had gone a little way, the wolves, who had been showing themselves on the edge of a neighboring coppice, came nearer, and the birds wheeled closer and closer. "Stay, outcasts, yet a little while," the crucified one called in a weak voice to the beggars, "and keep the beasts and the birds from me." But the beggars were angry because he had called them outcasts, so they threw stones and mud at him, and one that had a child held it up before his eyes and said that he was its father, and cursed him, and thereupon they left him. Then the wolves gathered at the foot of the cross, and the birds flew lower and lower. And presently the birds lighted all at once upon his head and arms and shoulders, and began to peck at him, and the wolves began to eat his feet."Outcasts," he moaned, "have you all turned against the outcast?"

Daniel O'Rourke
Thomas Crofton Croker

PEOPLE may have heard of the renowned adventures of Daniel O'Rourke, but how few are there who know that the cause of all his perils, above and below, was neither more nor less than his having slept under the walls of the Pooka's tower. I knew the man well. He lived at the bottom of Hungry Hill, just at the right-hand side of the road as you go toward Bantry. An old man was he, at the time he told me the story, with gray hair and red nose; and it was on the 25th of June, 1813, that I heard it from his own lips, as he sat smoking his pipe under the old poplar tree, on as fine an evening as ever shone from the sky. I was going to visit the caves in Dursey Island, having spent the morning at Glengariff.

"I am often *axed* to tell it, sir," said he, "so that this is not the first time. The master's son, you see, had come from beyond foreign parts in France and Spain, as young gentlemen used to go before Buonaparte or any such was heard of; and sure enough there was a dinner given to all the people on the ground, gentle and simple, high and low, rich and poor. The *ould* gentlemen were the gentlemen after all, saving your honor's presence. They'd swear at a body a little, to be sure, and, maybe, give one a cut of a whip now and then, but we were no losers by it in the end; and they were so easy and civil, and kept such rattling houses, and thousands of welcomes; and there was no grinding for rent, and there was hardly a tenant on the estate that did not taste of his landlord's bounty often and often in a year; but now it's another thing. No matter for that, sir, for I'd better be telling you my story.

"Well, we had everything of the best, and plenty of it; and we ate, and we drank and we danced, and the young master by the same token danced with Peggy Barry, from the *Bohereen*—a lovely young couple they were, though they are both low enough now. To make a long story short, I got, as a body may say, the same thing as tipsy almost, for I can't remember ever at all, no ways, how it was I left the place; only I did leave it, that's certain. Well, I thought for all that, in myself, I'd just step to Molly Cronohan's, the fairy woman, to speak a word about the bracket heifer that was bewitched; and so as I was crossing the stepping-stones of the ford of Ballyashenogh, and as looking up at the stars and blessing myself—for why? it was Lady-day—I missed my foot, and souse I fell into the water. 'Death alive!' thought I, 'I'll be drowned now!' However, I began swimming, swimming, swimming away for the dear life, till at last I got ashore, somehow or other, but never the one of me can tell how, upon a *dissolute* island.

"I wandered and wandered about there, without knowing where I wandered, until at last I got into a big bog. The moon was shining as bright as day, or your fair lady's eyes, sir (with the pardon for mentioning her), and I looked east and west, and north and south, and every way, and nothing did I see but bog, bog, bog—I could never find out how I got into it; and my heart grew cold with fear, for sure and certain I was that it would be my *berrin* place. So I sat down upon a stone which, as good luck would have it, was close by me, and I began to scratch my head, and sing the *Ullagone*—when all of a sudden the moon grew black, and I looked up, and saw something for all the world as if it was moving down between me and it, and I could not tell what it was. Down it came with a pounce, and looked at me full in the face; and what was it but an eagle? as fine a one as ever flew from the kingdom of Kerry. So he looked at me in the face, and says he to me, 'Daniel O'Rourke,' says he, 'how do you do?' 'Very well, I thank you, sir,' says I; 'I hope you're well'; wondering out of my senses all the time how an eagle came to speak like a Christian. 'What brings you here, Dan?' says he. 'Nothing at all, sir,' says I; 'only I wish I was safe home again.' 'Is it out of the island you want to go, Dan?' says he. ''Tis, sir,' says I: so I up and told him how I had taken a drop too much, and fell into the water; how I swam to the island; and how I got into the bog and did not know my way out of it. 'Dan,' says he, after a minute's thought, 'though it is very improper for you to get drunk on Lady-day, yet as you are a decent, sober man, who 'tends mass well and never flings stones at me or mine, nor cries out after us in the fields—my life for yours,' says he; 'so get up on my back, and grip me well for fear you'd fall off, and I'll fly you out of the bog.' 'I am afraid,' says I, 'your honor's making game of me; for who ever heard of riding horseback on an eagle before?' ''Pon the honor of a gentleman,' says he, putting his right foot on his breast, 'I am quite in earnest: and so now either take my offer or starve in the bog—besides, I see that your weight is sinking the stone.'

"It was true enough as he said, for I found the stone every minute going from under me. I had no choice; so thinks I to myself, faint heart never won fair lady, and this is fair persuadance. 'I thank your honor,' says I, 'for the loan of your civility; and I'll take your kind offer.'

"I therefore mounted upon the back of the eagle, and held him tight enough by the throat, and up he flew in the air like a lark. Little I knew the trick he was going to serve me. Up—up—up, God knows how far up he flew. 'Why then,' said I to him—thinking he did not know the right road home—very civilly, because why? I was in his power entirely; 'sir,' says I, 'please your honor's glory, and with humble submission to your better judgment, if you'd fly down a bit, you're now just over my cabin, and I could be put down there, and many thanks to your worship.'

"'*Arrah*, Dan,' said he, 'do you think me a fool? Look down the next field, and don't you see two men and a gun? By my word it would be no joke to be shot this way, to oblige a drunken blackguard that I picked up off of a *could* stone in a bog.' 'Bother you,' said I to myself, but I did not speak out, for where was the use? Well, sir, up he kept flying, flying, and I asking him every minute to fly down, and all to no use. 'Where in the world are you going, sir?' says I to him. 'Hold your tongue, Dan,' says he: 'mind your own business, and don't be interfering with the business of other people.' 'Faith, this is my business, I think,' says I. 'Be quiet, Dan,' says he: so I said no more.

"At last where should we come to, but to the moon itself. Now you can't see it from this, but there is, or there was in my time, a reaping-hook sticking out of the side of the moon, this way (drawing the figure thus, Ω, on the ground with the end of his stick).

"'Dan,' said the eagle, 'I'm tired with this long fly; I had no notion 'twas so far.' 'And my lord, sir,' said I, 'who in the world *axed* you to fly so far—was it I? Did not I beg and pray and beseech you to stop half an hour ago?' 'There's no use talking, Dan,' said he; 'I'm tired bad enough, so you must get off, and sit down on the moon until I rest myself.' 'Is it sit down on the moon?' said I, 'is it upon that little round thing, then? why, then, sure I'd fall off in a minute, and be *kilt* and spilt and smashed all to bits; you are a vile deceiver—so you are.' 'Not at all, Dan, said he; 'you can catch fast hold of the reaping-hook that's sticking out of the side of the moon, and 'twill keep you up.' 'I won't then,' said I. 'Maybe not,' said he, quite quiet. 'If you don't, my man, I shall just give you a shake, and one slap of my wing, and send you down to the ground, where every bone in your body will be smashed as small as a drop of dew on a cabbage-leaf in the morning.' 'Why, then, I'm in a fine way,' said I to myself, 'ever to have come along with the likes of you;' and so giving him a hearty curse in Irish, for fear he'd know what I said, I got off his back with a heavy heart, took hold of the reaping hook, and sat down upon the moon, and a mighty cold seat it was, I can tell you that.

"When he had me there fairly landed, he turned about on me, and said: 'Good morning to you, Daniel O'Rourke,' said he; "I think I've nicked you fairly now. You robbed my nest last year' ('twas true enough for him, but how he found it out is hard to say), 'and in return you are freely welcome to cool your heels dangling upon the moon like a cockthrow.'

"'Is that all, and is this the way you leave me, you brute, you,' says I. 'You ugly, unnatural *baste*, and is this the way you serve me at last? Bad luck to yourself, with your hook'd nose, and to all your breed, you blackguard.' 'Twas all to no manner of use;

he spread out his great big wings, burst out a-laughing, and flew away like lightning. I bawled after him to stop; but I might have called and bawled for ever, without his minding me. Away he went, and I never saw him from that day to this sorrow fly away with him! You may be sure I was in a disconsolate condition, and kept roaring out for the bare grief, when all at once a door opened right in the middle of the moon, creaking on its hinges as if it had not been opened for a month before, I suppose they never thought of greasing 'em, and out there walks—who do you think, but the man in the moon himself? I knew him by his bush.

"'Good-morrow to you, Daniel O'Rourke,' said he; 'how do you do?' 'Very well, thank your honor,' said I. 'I hope your honor's well.' 'What brought you here, Dan?' said he. So I told him how I was a little overtaken in liquor at the master's, and how I was cast on a dissolute island, and how I lost my way in the bog, and how the thief of an eagle promised to fly me out of it and how, instead of that, he had fled me up to the moon.

"'Dan,' said the man in the moon, taking a pinch of snuff when I was done, 'you must not stay here.' 'Indeed, sir,' says I, ''tis much against my will I'm here at all; but how am I to go back?' 'That's your business,' said he; 'Dan, mine is to tell you that here you must not stay; so be off in less than no time.' 'I'm doing no harm,' says I, 'only holding on hard by the reaping-hook, lest I fall off.' 'That's what you must not do, Dan,' says he. 'Pray, sir,' say I, 'may I ask how many you are in family, that you would not give a poor traveler lodging: I'm sure 'tis not so often you're troubled with strangers coming to see you, for 'tis a long way.' 'I'm by myself, Dan,' says he; 'but you'd better let go the reaping-hook.' 'Faith, and with your leave,' says I, 'I'll not let go the grip, and the more you bid me, the more I won't let go;—so I will.' 'You had better, Dan,' says he again.

'why, then, my little fellow,' says I, taking the whole weight of him with my eye from head to foot, 'there are two words to that bargain; and I'll not budge, but you may if you like.' 'We'll see how that is to be,' says he; and back he went, giving the door such a great bang after him (for it was plain he was huffed) that I thought the moon and all would fall down with it.

"Well, I was preparing myself to try strength with him, when back again he comes, with the kitchen cleaver in his hand, and, without saying a word, he gives two bangs to the handle of the reaping-hook that was keeping me up, and *whap*! it came in two. 'Good-morning to you, Dan,' says the spiteful little old blackguard, when he saw me cleanly falling down with a bit of the handle in my hand; I thank you for your visit and fair weather after you, Daniel.' I had not time to make answer to him, for I was tumbling over and over and rolling and rolling, at the rate of a fox-hunt. 'God help me!' says I, 'but this is a pretty pickle for a decent man to be seen in at this time of night: I am now sold fairly.' The word was not out of my mouth when, *whiz*! what should fly by close to my ear but a flock of wild geese, all the way from my own bog of Ballyasheenogh, else how should they know *me*? The *ould* gander, who was their general, turning about his head, cried out to me, 'Is that you, Dan?' 'The same,' said I, not a bit daunted now at what he said, for I was by this time used to all kinds of *bedevilment*, and, besides, I knew him of ould. 'Good-morrow to you,' says he, 'Daniel O'Rourke; how are you in health this morning?' 'Very well, sir,' says I, 'I thank you kindly,' drawing my breath, for I was mightily in want of some. 'I hope your honor's the same.' 'I think 'tis falling you are, Daniel,' says he. 'You may say that, sir,' says I. 'And where are you going all the way so fast?' said the gander. So I told him how I had taken the drop, and how I came on the island, and how I lost my way in the bog, and how the thief of an eagle flew me up to the moon, and how the man in the moon turned me out. 'Dan,' said he, 'I'll save you: put out your hand and catch me by the leg, and I'll fly you home.' 'Sweet is your hand in a pitcher of honey, my jewel,' says I, though all the time I thought within myself that I don't much trust you; but there was no help, so I caught the gander by the leg, and away I and the other geese flew after him fast as hops.

"We flew, and we flew, and we flew, until we came right over the wide ocean. I knew it well, for I saw Cape Clear to my right hand, sticking up out of the water. 'Ah, my lord,' said I to the goose, for I thought it best to keep a civil tongue in my head anyway, 'fly to land if you please.' 'It is impossible, you see, Dan'; said he, 'for a while, because you see we are going to Arabia.' 'To Arabia!' said I; 'that's surely some place in foreign parts, far away. Oh! Mr. Goose: why then, to be sure, I'm a man to be pitied among you.' 'Whist, whist, you fool,' said he, 'hold your tongue; I tell you Arabia is a very decent sort of place, as like West Carbery as one egg is like another, only there is a little more sand there.'

"Just as we were talking, a ship hove in sight, scudding so beautiful before the wind. 'Ah! then, sir,' said I, 'will you drop me on the ship, if you please?' 'We are not fair over it,' said he; 'if I dropped you now you would go splash into the sea.' 'I would not,' says I; 'I know better than that, for it is just clean under us, so let me drop now at once.'

"'If you must, you must,' said he; 'there, take your way'; and he opened his claw, and faith he was right—sure enough I came down plump into the very bottom of the salt sea! Down to the very bottom I went, and I gave myself up then forever, when a whale walked up to me, scratching himself after his night's sleep, and looked me full in the face, and never the word did he say, but lifting up his tail, he splashed me all over again with the cold salt water till there wasn't a dry stitch upon my whole carcass! and I heard somebody saying—'twas a voice I knew, too—'Get up, you drunken brute, off o' that,' and with that I woke up and there was Judy with a tub full of water, which she was splashing all over me for, rest her soul! though she was a good wife, she never could bear to see me in drink, and had a bitter hand of her own.

"'Get up,' said she again: 'and of all places in the parish would no place *sarve* your turn to lie down upon but under the *ould* walls of Carrigapooka? an *uneasy* resting I am sure you had of it.' And sure enough I had: for I was fairly bothered out of my senses with eagles, and men of the moons, and flying ganders, and whales, driving me through bogs, and up to the moon, and down to the bottom of the green ocean. If I was in drink ten times over, long would it be before I'd lie down in the same spot again, I know that."

The Eyes of the Dead
Daniel Corkery

I

IF HE had not put it off for three years John Spillane's homecoming would have been that of a famous man. Bonfires would have been lighted on the hill-tops of Rossamara, and the ships passing by, twenty miles out, would have wondered what they meant.

Three years ago, the *Western Star*, an Atlantic liner, one night tore her iron plates to pieces against the cliff-like face of an iceberg, and in less than an hour sank in the waters. Of the 789 human souls aboard her one only had been saved, John Spillane, able seaman, of Rossamara in the county of Cork. The name of the little fishing village, his own name, his picture, were in all the papers of the world, it seemed, not only because he alone had escaped, but by reason of the manner of that escape. He had clung to a drift of wreckage, must have lost consciousness for more than a whole day, floated then about on the ocean for a second day, for a second night, and had arrived at the threshold of another dreadful night when he was rescued. A fog was coming down on the waters. It frightened him more than the darkness. He raised a shout. He kept on shouting. When safe in the arms of his rescuers his breathy, almost inaudible voice was still forcing out some cry which they interpreted as Help! Help!

That was what had struck the imagination of men—the half-insane figure sending his cry over the waste of waters, the fog thickening, and the night falling. Although the whole world had read also of the groping rescue ship, of Spillane's bursts of hysterical laughter, of his inability to tell his story until he had slept eighteen hours on end, what remained in the memory was the lonely figure sending his cry over the sea.

And then, almost before his picture had disappeared from the papers, he had lost himself in the great cities of the States. To Rossamara no word had come from himself, nor for a long time from any acquaintance; but then, when about a year had gone by, his sister or mother as they went up the road to Mass of a Sunday might be stopped and informed in a whispering voice that John had been seen in Chicago, or, it might be, in New York, or Boston, or San Francisco, or indeed anywhere. And from the meagerness of the messages it was known, with only too much certainty, that he had not, in exchanging sea for land, bettered his lot. If once again his people had happened on such empty tidings of him, one knew it by their bowed and stilly attitude in the little church as the light whisper of the Mass rose and fell about them.

When three years had gone by he lifted the latch of his mother's house one October evening and stood awkwardly in the middle of the floor. It was nightfall and not a soul had seen him break down from the ridge and cross the roadway. He had come secretly from the ends of the earth.

And before he was an hour in their midst he rose up impatiently, timidly, and stole into his bed.

"I don't want any light," he said, and as his mother left him there in the dark, she heard him yield his whole being to a sigh of thankfulness. Before that he had told them he felt tired, a natural thing, since he had tramped fifteen miles from the railway station in Skibbereen. But day followed day without his showing any desire to rise from the bedclothes and go abroad among the people. He had had enough of the sea, it seemed; enough too of the great cities of the States. He was a pity, the neighbors said; and the few of them who from time to time caught glimpses of him, reported him as not yet having lost the scared look that the ocean had left on him. His hair was grey or nearly grey, they said, and, swept back fiercely from his forehead, a fashion strange to the place, seemed to pull his eyes open, to keep them wide open, as he looked at you. His moustache also was grey, they said, and his cheeks were grey too, sunken and dark with shadows. Yet his mother and sister, the only others in the house, were glad to have him back with them; at any rate, they said, they knew where he was.

They found nothing wrong with him. Of speech neither he nor they ever had had the gift; and as day followed day, and week week, the same few phrases would carry them through the day and into the silence of night. In the beginning they had thought it natural to speak with him about the wreck; soon, however, they came to know that it was a subject for which he had no welcome. In the beginning also, they had thought to rouse him by bringing the neighbor to his bedside, but such visits instead of cheering him only left him sunken in silence, almost in despair. The priest came to see him once in a while, and advised the mother and sister, Mary her name was, to treat him as normally as they could, letting on that his useless presence was no affliction to them nor even a burden. In time John Spillane was accepted by all as one of those unseen ones, or seldom-seen ones, who are to be found in every village in the world—the bedridden, the struck-down, the aged—forgotten of all except the few faithful creatures who bring the cup to the bedside of a morning, and open the curtains to let in the sun.

II

In the nearest house, distant a quarter-mile from them, lived Tom Leane. In the old days before John Spillane went to sea, Tom had been his companion, and now of a night-time he would drop in if he had any story worth telling or if, on the day following, he chanced to be going back to Skibbereen, where he might buy the Spillanes such goods as they needed, or sell a pig for them, slipping it in among his own. He was a quiet creature, married, and struggling to bring up the little family that was thickening about him. In the Spillanes' he would, dragging at the pipe, sit on the settle, and quietly gossip with the old woman while Mary moved about on the flags putting the household gear tidy for the night. But all three of them, as they kept up the simple talk, were never unaware of the silent listener in the lower room. Of that room the door was kept open; but no lamp was lighted within it; no lamp indeed was needed, for a shaft of light from the kitchen struck into it showing one or two of the religious pictures on the wall and giving sufficient light to move about in. Sometimes the conversation would drift away from the neighborly doings, for even to Rossamara tidings from the great world abroad would sometimes come; in the middle of such gossip, however, a sudden thought would strike Tom Leane, and, raising his voice, he would blurt out: "But sure 'tis foolish for the like of me to be talking about these far-off places, and that man inside after traveling the world, over and thither." The man inside, however, would give no sign whatever whether their gossip had been wise or foolish. They might hear the bed creak, as if he had turned with impatience at their mention of his very presence.

There had been a spell of stormy weather, it was now the middle of February, and for the last five days at twilight the gale seemed always to set in for a night of it. Although there was scarcely a house around that part of the southwest Irish coast that had not some one of its members, husband or brother or son, living on the sea, sailoring abroad or fishing the home waters or those of the Isle of Man—in no other house was the strain of a spell of disastrous weather so noticeable in the faces of its inmates. The old woman, withdrawn into herself, would handle her beads all day long, her voice every now and then raising itself, in forgetfulness, to a sort of moan not unlike the wind's, upon which the younger woman would chide her with a "Sh! sh!" and bend vigorously upon her work to keep bitterness from her thoughts. At such a time she might enter her brother's room and find him raised on his elbow in the bed, listening to the howling winds, scared it seemed, his eyes fixed and wide open. He would drink the warm milk she had brought him, and hand the vessel back without a word. And in the selfsame attitude she would leave him.

The fifth night instead of growing in loudness and fierceness the wind died away somewhat. It became fitful, promising the end of the storm; and before long they could distinguish between the continuous groaning and pounding of the sea and the sudden shout the dying tempest would fling among the treetops and the rocks. They were thankful to note such signs of relief; the daughter became more active, and the mother put by her beads. In the midst of a sudden sally of the wind's the latch was raised, and Tom Leane gave them greeting. His face was rosy and glowing under his sou'wester; his eyes were sparkling from the sting of the salty gusts. To see him, so sane, so healthy, was to them like a blessing. "How is it with ye?" he said, cheerily, closing the door to.

"Good, then, good, then," they answered him, and the mother rose almost as if she would take him by the hand. The reply meant that nothing unforeseen had befallen them. He understood as much. He shook a silent head in the direction of the listener's room, a look of inquiry in his eyes, and this look Mary answered with a sort of hopeless upswing of her face. Things had not improved in the lower room.

The wind died away, more and more; and after some time streamed by with a shrill steady undersong; all through, however, the crashing of the sea on the jagged rocks beneath kept up an unceasing clamor. Tom had a whole budget of news for them. Finny's barn had been stripped of its roof; a window in the chapel had been blown in; and Largy's store of fodder had been shredded in the wind; it littered all the bushes to the east. There were rumors of a wreck somewhere; but it was too soon yet to know what damage the sea had done in its five days' madness. The news he had brought them did not matter; what mattered was his company, the knitting of their half-distraught household once again to humankind. Even when at last he stood up to go, their spirits did not droop, so great had been the restoration.

"We're finished with it for a while anyhow," Tom said, rising for home.

"We are, we are; and who knows, it mightn't be after doing

all the damage we think."

He shut the door behind him. The two women had turned towards the fire when they thought they again heard his voice outside. They wondered at the sound; they listened for his footsteps. Still staring at the closed door, once more they heard his voice. This time they were sure. The door reopened, and he backed in, as one does from an unexpected slap of rain in the face. The light struck outwards, and they saw a white face advancing. Some anxiety, some uncertainty, in Tom's attitude as he backed away from that advancing face, invaded them so that they too became afraid. They saw the stranger also hesitating, looking down his own limbs. His clothes were dripping; they were clung in about him. He was bare-headed. When he raised his face again, his look was full of apology. His features were large and flat, and grey as a stone. Every now and then a spasm went through them, and they wondered what it meant. His clab of a mouth hung open; his unshaven chin trembled. Tom spoke to him: "You'd better come in; but 'tis many another house would suit you better than this."

They heard a husky, scarce-audible voice reply: "A doghouse would do, or a stable." Bravely enough he made an effort to smile.

"Oh, 'tisn't that at all. But come in, come in." He stepped in slowly and heavily, again glancing down his limbs. The water running from his clothes spread in a black pool on the flags. The young woman began to touch him with her finger tips as with some instinctive sympathy, yet could not think, it seemed, what was best to be done. The mother, however, vigorously set the fire-wheel at work, and Tom built up the fire with bog-timber and turf. The stranger meanwhile stood as if half-dazed. At last, as Mary with a candle in her hand stood pulling out dry clothes from a press, he blurted out in the same husky voice, Welsh in accent:

"I think I'm the only one!"

They understood the significance of the words, but it seemed wrong to do so.

"What is it you're saying?" Mary said, but one would not have recognized the voice for hers, it was so toneless. He raised a heavy sailor's hand in an awkward taproom gesture: "The others, they're gone, all of them."

The spasm again crossed his homely features, and his hand fell. He bowed his head. A coldness went through them. They stared at him. He might have thought them inhuman. But Mary suddenly pulled herself together, leaping at him almost: "Sh! Sh!" she said, "speak low, speak low, low," and as she spoke, all earnestness, she towed him first in the direction of the fire, and then away from it, haphazardly it seemed. She turned from him and whispered to Tom:

"Look, take him up into the loft, and he can change his clothes. Take these with you, and the candle, the candle." And she reached him the candle eagerly. Tom led the stranger up the stairs, it was more like a ladder, and the two of them disappeared into the loft. The old woman whispered:

"What was it he said?"

"'Tis how his ship is sunk."

"Did he say he was the only one?"

"He said that."

"Did himself hear him?" She nodded towards her son's room.

"No, didn't you see me pulling him away from it? But he'll hear him now. Isn't it a wonder Tom wouldn't walk easy on the boards!"

No answer from the old woman. She had deliberately seated herself in her accustomed place at the fire, and now moaned out:

"Aren't we in a cruel way, not knowing how he'd take a

thing!"

"Am I better tell him there's a poor seaman after coming in on us?"

"Do you hear them above! Do you hear them!"

In the loft the men's feet were loud on the boards. The voice they were half-expecting to hear they then heard break in on the clatter of the boots above:

"Mother! Mother!"

"Yes, child, yes."

"Who's aloft? Who's going around like that, or is it dreaming I am?"

The sounds from above were certainly like what one hears in a ship. They thought of this, but they also felt something terrible in that voice they had been waiting for: they hardly knew it for the voice of the man they had been listening to for five months.

"Go in and tell him the truth," the mother whispered. "Who are we to know what's right to be done. Let God have the doing of it." She threw her hands in the air.

Mary went in to her brother, and her limbs were weak and cold. The old woman remained seated at the fire, swung round from it, her eyes towards her son's room, fixed, as the head itself was fixed, in the tension of anxiety.

After a few minutes Mary emerged with a strange alertness upon her:

"He's rising! He's getting up! 'Tis his place, he says. He's quite good." She meant he seemed bright and well. The mother said:

"We'll take no notice of him, only just as if he was always with us."

"Yes."

They were glad then to hear the two men in the loft groping for the stair head. The kettle began to splutter in the boil, and

Mary busied herself with the table and tea cups.

The sailor came down, all smiles in his ill-fitting, haphazard clothes. He looked so overjoyed one might think he would presently burst into song.

III

"The fire is good," he said. "It puts life in one. And the dry clothes too. My word, I'm thankful to you, good people; I'm thankful to you." He shook hands with them all effusively.

"Sit down now; drink up the tea."

"I can't figure it out; less than two hours ago, out there . . . As he spoke he raised his hand towards the little porthole of a window, looking at them with his eyes staring. "Don't be thinking of anything, but drink up the hot tea," Mary said.

He nodded and set to eat with vigor. Yet suddenly he would stop, as if he were ashamed of it, turn half-round and look at them with beaming eyes, look from one to the other and back again; and they affably would nod back at him. "Excuse me, people," he would say, "excuse me." He had not the gift of speech, and his too-full heart could not declare itself. To make him feel at his ease, Tom Leane sat down away from him, and the women began to find something to do about the room. Then there were only little sounds in the room: the breaking of the eggs, the turning of the fire-wheel, the wind going by. The door of the lower room opened silently, so silently that none of them heard it, and before they were aware, the son of the house, with his clothes flung on loosely, was standing awkwardly in the middle of the floor, looking down on the back of the sailorman bent above the table. "This is my son," the mother thought of saying. "He was after going to bed when you came in."

The Welshman leaped to his feet, and impulsively, yet without many words, shook John Spillane by the hand, thanking him and all the household. As he seated himself again at the table John made his way silently towards the settle from which, across the room, he could see the sailor as he bent over his meal.

The stranger put the cup away from him, he could take no more; and Tom Leane and the womenfolk tried to keep him in talk, avoiding, as by some mutual understanding, the mention of what he had come through. The eyes of the son of the house were all the time fiercely buried in him. There came a moment's silence in the general chatter, a moment it seemed impossible to fill, and the sailorman swung his chair half-round from the table, a spoon held in his hand lightly: "I can't figure it out. I can't nohow figure it out. Here I am, fed full like a prize beast; and warm—Oh, but I'm thankful—and all my mates," with the spoon he was pointing towards the sea—"white, and cold like dead fish! I can't figure it out."

To their astonishment a voice traveled across the room from the settle

"Is it how ye struck?"

"Struck! Three times we struck! We struck last night, about this time last night. And off we went in a puff! Fine, we said. We struck again. 'Twas just coming light. And off again. But when we struck the third time, 'twas like that!" He clapped his hands together; "She went in matchwood! 'Twas dark. Why, it can't be two hours since!"

"She went to pieces?" the same voice questioned him.

"The *Nan Tidy* went to pieces, sir! No one knew what had happened or where he was. 'Twas too sudden. I found myself clung about a snag of rock. I hugged it. I hugged it."

He stood up, hoisted as from within.

"Is it you that was on the look-out?"

"Me! We'd all been on the look-out for three days. My word, yes, three days. We were stupefied with it!"

They were looking at him as he spoke, and they saw the shiver again cross his features; the strength and warmth that the food and comfort had given him fell from him, and he became in an instant the half-drowned man who had stepped in to them that night with the clothes sagging about his limbs, "Twas bad, clinging to that rock, with them all gone! 'Twas lonely! Do you know, I was so frightened I couldn't call out." John Spillane stood up, slowly, as if he too were being hoisted from within.

"Were they looking at you?"

"Who?"

"The rest of them. The eyes of them."

"No," the voice had dropped, "no, I didn't think of that!" The two of them stared as if fascinated by each other.

"You didn't!" It seemed that John Spillane had lost the purpose of his questioning. His voice was thin and weak; but he was still staring with unmoving, puzzled eyes at the stranger's face. The abashed creature before him suddenly seemed to gain as much eagerness as he had lost: his words were hot with anxiety to express himself adequately:

"But now, isn't it curious, as I sat there, there at that table, I thought somehow they would walk in, that it would be right for them, somehow, to walk in, all of them!"

His words, his eager lowered voice, brought in the darkness outside, its vastness, its terror. They seemed in the midst of an unsubstantial world. They feared that the latch would lift, yet dared not glance at it, lest that should invite the lifting. But it was all one to the son of the house, he appeared to have gone away into some mood of his own; his eyes were glaring, not looking at anything or anyone close at hand. With an instinctive groping for comfort, they all, except him, began to stir, to find some little homely task to do: Mary handled the tea ware, and Tom his pipe, when a rumbling voice, very indistinct, stilled them all again. Words, phrases, began to reach them—that a man's eyes will close and he on the lookout, close in spite of himself, that it wasn't fair, it wasn't fair, it wasn't fair! And lost in his agony, he began to glide through them, explaining, excusing the terror that was in him: "All round. Staring at me. Blaming me. A sea of them. Far, far! Without a word out of them, only their eyes in the darkness, pale like candles!"

Transfixed, they glared at him, at his round-shouldered sailor's back disappearing again into his den of refuge. They could not hear his voice any more, they were afraid to follow him.

The Three Wishes
William Carleton

IN ANCIENT TIMES there lived a man called Billy Dawson, and he was known to be a great rogue. They say he was descended from the family of the Dawsons, which was the reason, I suppose, of his carrying their name upon him.

Billy, in his youthful days, was the best hand at doing nothing in all Europe; devil a mortal could come next or near him at idleness; and, in consequence of his great practice that way, you may be sure that if any man could make a fortune by it he would have done it.

Billy was the only son of his father, barring two daughters, but they have nothing to do with the story I'm telling you. Indeed it was kind father and grandfather for Billy to be handy at the knavery as well as at the idleness, for it was well known that not one of their blood ever did an honest act, except with a roguish intention. In short, they were altogether a *dacent* connection and a credit to the name. As for Billy, all the villainy of the family, both plain and ornamental, came down to him by way of legacy, for it so happened that the father, in spite of all his cleverness, had nothing but his roguery to *lave* him.

Billy, to do him justice, improved the fortune he got. Every day advanced him farther into dishonesty and poverty, until, at the long run, he was acknowledged on all hands to be the completest swindler and the poorest vagabond in the whole parish.

Billy's father, in his young days, had often been forced to acknowledge the inconvenience of not having a trade, in consequence of some nice point in law, called the "Vagrant Act," that sometimes troubled him. On this account he made up his mind to give Bill an occupation, and he accordingly bound him to a blacksmith; but whether Bill was to *live* or *die* by *forgery* was a puzzle to his father—though the neighbors said that *both* was most likely. At all events, he was put apprentice to a smith for seven years, and a hard card his master had to play in managing him. He took the proper method, however, for Bill was so lazy and roguish that it would vex a saint to keep him in order.

"Bill," says his master to him one day that he had been sunning himself about the ditches, instead of minding his business, "Bill, my boy, I'm vexed to the heart to see you in such a bad state of health. You're very ill with that complaint called an *all-overness*; however," says he, "I think I can cure you. Nothing will bring you about but three or four sound doses every day of a medicine called 'the oil o' the hazel.' Take the first dose now," says he, and he immediately banged him with a hazel cudgel until Bill's bones ached for a week afterward.

"If you were my son," said his master, "I tell you that, as long as I could get a piece of advice growing convenient in the hedges, I'd have you a different youth from what you are. If working was a sin, Bill, not an innocenter boy ever broke bread than you would be. Good people's scarce, you think; but however that may be, I throw it out as a hint, that you must take your medicine till you're cured, whenever you happen to get unwell in the same way."

From this out he kept Bill's nose to the grinding stone, and whenever his complaint returned he never failed to give him a hearty dose for his improvement.

In the course of time, however, Bill was his own man and his own master, but it would puzzle a saint to know whether the master or the man was the more precious youth in the eyes of the world.

He immediately married a wife, and devil a doubt of it, but if *he* kept *her* in whisky and sugar, *she* kept *him* in hot water. Bill drank and she drank; Bill fought and she fought; Bill was idle and she was idle; Bill whacked her and she whacked Bill. If Bill gave her one black eye, she gave him another, *just to keep herself in countenance*. Never was there a blessed pair so well met, and a beautiful sight it was to see them both at breakfast time, blinking at each other across the potato basket, Bill with his right eye black, and she with her left.

In short, they were the talk of the whole town; and to see Bill of a morning staggering home drunk, his shirt sleeves rolled up on his smutted arms, his breast open, and an old tattered leather apron, with one corner tucked up under his belt, singing one minute and fighting with his wife the next—she, reeling beside him with a discolored eye, as aforesaid, a dirty ragged cap on one side of her head, a pair of Bill's old slippers on her feet, a squalling child on her arm—now cuffing and dragging Bill, and again kissing and hugging him! Yes, it was a pleasant picture to see this loving pair in such a state!

This might do for a while, but it could not last. They were idle, drunken, and ill conducted; and it was not to be supposed that they would get a farthing candle on their words. They were, of course, *druv* to great straits; and faith, they soon found that their fighting and drinking and idleness made them the laughing sport of the neighbors; but neither brought food to their *childhre*, put a coat upon their backs, nor satisfied their landlord when he came to look for his own. Still, the never a one of Bill but was a funny fellow with strangers, though, as we said, the greatest rogue unhanged.

One day he was standing against his own anvil, completely in a brown study—being brought to his wit's end how to make out a breakfast for the family. The wife was scolding and cursing in the house, and the naked creatures of children squalling about her knees for food. Bill was fairly at an amplush, and knew not where or how to turn himself, when a poor, withered old beggar came into the forge, tottering on his staff. A long white beard fell from his chin, and he looked as thin and hungry that you might blow him, one would think, over the house. Bill at this moment had been brought to his senses by distress, and his heart had a touch of pity toward the old man, for, on looking at him a second time, he clearly saw starvation and sorrow in his face.

"God save you, honest man!" said Bill.

The old man gave a sigh, and raising himself with great pain on his staff, he looked at Bill in a very beseeching way.

"Musha, God save you kindly!" says he. "Maybe you could give a poor, hungry, helpless ould man a mouthful of something to ait? You see yourself I'm not able to work; if I was, I'd scorn to be beholding to anyone."

"Faith, honest man," said Bill, "if you knew who you're speaking to, you'd as soon ask a monkey for a churnstaff as me for either mate or money. There's not a blackguard in the three kingdoms so fairly on the *shaughran* as I am for both the one and the other. The wife within is sending the curses thick and heavy on me, and the *childhre's* playing the cat's melody to keep her in comfort. Take my word for it, poor man, if I had either mate or money I'd help you, for I know particularly well what it is to want them at the present speaking; an empty sack won't stand, neighbor."

So far Bill told him truth. The good thought was in his heart, because he found himself on a footing with the beggar; and nothing brings down pride, or softens the heart, like feeling what it is to want.

"Why, you are in a worse state than I am," said the old man; "you have a family to provide for, and I have only myself to support."

"You may kiss the book on that, my old worthy," replied Bill; "but come, what I can do for you I will; plant yourself up here beside the fire, and I'll give it a blast or two of my bellows that will warm the old blood in your body. It's a cold, miserable, snowy day, and a good heat will be of service."

"Thank you kindly," said the old man; "I *am* cold, and a warming at your fire will do me good, sure enough. Oh, but it *is* a bitter, bitter day; God bless it!"

He then sat down, and Bill blew a rousing blast that soon made the stranger edge back from the heat. In a short time he felt quite comfortable, and when the numbness was taken out of his joints, he buttoned himself up and prepared to depart.

"Now," says he to Bill, "you hadn't the food to give me, but *what you could you did*. Ask any three wishes you choose, and be they what they may, take my word for it, they shall be granted."

Now, the truth is, that Bill, though he believed himself a great man in point of 'cuteness, wanted, after all, a full quarter of being square, for there is always a great difference between a wise man and a knave. Bill was so much of a rogue that he could not, for the blood of him, ask an honest wish, but stood scratching his head in a puzzle.

"Three wishes!" said he. "Why, let me see—did you say *three*?"

"Ay," replied the stranger, "three wishes—that was what I said."

"Well," said Bill, "here goes—aha!—let me alone, my old worthy!—faith I'll overreach the parish, if what you say is true. I'll cheat them in dozens, rich and poor, old and young; let me alone, man—I have it here," and he tapped his forehead with great glee. "Faith, you're the sort to meet of a frosty morning, when a man wants his breakfast; and I'm sorry that I have neither money nor credit to get a bottle of whisky, that we might take our morning together."

"Well, but let us hear the wishes," said the old man; "my time is short, and I cannot stay much longer."

"Do you see this sledge hammer?" said Bill. "I wish, in the first place, that whoever takes it up in their hands may never be able to lay it down till I give them lave; and that whoever begins to sledge with it may never stop sledging till it's my pleasure to release him.

"Secondly—I have an armchair, and I wish that whoever sits down in it may never rise out of it till they have my consent.

"And, thirdly—that whatever money I put into my purse, nobody may have power to take it out of it but myself!"

"You Devil's rip!" says the old man in a passion, shaking his staff across Bill's nose. "Why did you not ask something that would sarve you both here and hereafter? Sure it's as common as the market cross, that there's not a vagabone in His Majesty's dominions stands more in need of both."

"Oh! By the elevens," said Bill, "I forgot that altogether! Maybe you'd be civil enough to let me change one of them? The sorra purtier wish ever was made than I'll make, if only you'll give me another chance at it."

"Get out, you reprobate," said the old fellow, still in a passion. "Your day of grace is past. Little you knew who was speaking to you all this time. I'm St. Moroky, you blackguard, and I gave you an opportunity of doing something for yourself and your family; but you neglected it, and now your fate is cast, you dirty, bog-trotting profligate. Sure, it's well known what you are! Aren't you a byword in everybody's mouth, you and your scold of a wife? By this and by that, if ever you happen to come across me again, I'll send you to where you won't freeze, you villain!"

He then gave Bill a rap of his cudgel over the head and laid him at his length beside the bellows, kicked a broken coal scuttle out of his way, and left the forge in a fury.

When Billy recovered himself from the effects of the blow and began to think on what had happened, he could have quartered himself with vexation for not asking great wealth as one of the wishes at least; but now the die was cast on him, and he could only make the most of the three he pitched upon.

He now bethought him how he might turn them to the best account, and here his cunning came to his aid. He began by sending for his wealthiest neighbors on pretence of business, and when he got them under his roof he offered them the armchair to sit down in. He now had them safe, nor could all the art of man relieve them except worthy Bill was willing. Bill's plan was to make the best bargain he could before he released his prisoners; and let him alone for knowing how to make their purses bleed. There wasn't a wealthy man in the country he did not fleece. The parson of the parish bled heavily; so did the lawyer; and a rich attorney, who had retired from practice, swore that the Court of Chancery itself was paradise compared to Bill's chair.

This was all very good for a time. The fame of his chair, however, soon spread; so did that of his sledge. In a short time neither man, woman, nor child would darken his door; all avoided him and his fixtures as they would a spring gun or mantrap. Bill, so long as he fleeced his neighbors, never wrought a hand's turn; so that when his money was out he found himself as badly off as ever. In addition to all this, his character was fifty times worse than before, for it was the general belief that he had dealings with the old boy. Nothing now could exceed his misery, distress, and ill temper. The wife and he and their children all fought among one another. Everybody hated them, cursed them, and avoided them. The people thought they were acquainted with more than Christian people ought to know. This, of course, came to Bill's ears, and it vexed him very much.

One day he was walking about the fields, thinking of how he could raise the wind once more; the day was dark, and he found himself, before he stopped, in the bottom of a lonely glen covered by great bushes that grew on each side. "Well," thought he, when every other means of raising money failed him, "it's reported that I'm in league with the old boy, and as it's a folly to have the name of the connection without the profit, I'm ready to make a bargain with him any day—so," said he, raising his voice, "Nick, you sinner, if you be convanient and willing why stand out here; show your best leg—here's your man."

The words were hardly out of his mouth when a dark, sober-looking old gentleman, not unlike a lawyer, walked up to him. Bill looked at the foot and saw the hoof. "Morrow, Nick," says

Bill.

"Morrow, Bill," says Nick. "Well, Bill, what's the news?"

"Devil a much myself hears of late," says Bill; "is there anything *fresh* below?"

"I can't exactly say, Bill; I spend little of my time down now; the Tories are in office, and my hands are consequently too full of business here to pay much attention to anything else."

"A fine place this, sir," says Bill, "to take a constitutional walk in; when I want an appetite I often come this way myself—hem! *High* feeding is very bad without exercise."

"High feeding! Come, come, Bill, you know you didn't taste a morsel these four-and-twenty hours."

"You know that's a bounce, Nick. I ate a breakfast this morning that would put a stone of flesh on you, if you only smelt at it."

"No matter; this is not to the purpose. What's that you were muttering to yourself a while ago? If you want to come to the brunt, here I'm for you."

"Nick," said Bill, "you're complate; you want nothing barring a pair of Brian O'Lynn's breeches."

Bill, in fact, was bent on making his companion open the bargain, because he had often heard that, in that case, with proper care on his own part, he might defeat him in the long run. The other, however, was his match.

"What was the nature of Brian's garment?" inquired Nick.

"Why, you know the song," said Bill:

Brian O'Lynn had no breeches to wear,
So he got a sheep's skin for to make him a pair;
With the fleshy side out and the wooly side in,
'They'll be pleasant and cool,' says Brian O'Lynn.

"A cool pare would sarve you, Nick."

"You're mighty waggish today, Misther Dawson."

"And good right I have," said Bill; "I'm a man snug and well to do in the world; have lots of money, plenty of good eating and drinking, and what more need a man wish for?"

"True," said the other; "in the meantime it's rather odd that so respectable a man should not have six inches of unbroken cloth in his apparel. You're as naked a tatterdemalion as I ever laid my eyes on; in full dress for a party of scarecrows, William?"

"That's my own fancy, Nick; I don't work at my trade like a gentleman. This is my forge dress, you know."

"Well, but what did you summon me here for?" said the other; "you may as well speak out, I tell you, for, my good friend, unless you do, I shan't. Smell that."

"I smell more than that," said Bill; "and by the way, I'll thank you to give me the windy side of you—curse all sulphur, I say. There, that's what I call an improvement in my condition. But as you *are* so stiff," says Bill, "why, the short and long of it is—that—ahem—you see I'm—tut—sure you know I have a thriving trade of my own, and that if I like I needn't be at a loss; but in the meantime I'm rather in a kind of a so—so—don't you *take*?"

And Bill winked knowingly, hoping to trick him into the first proposal.

"You must speak aboveboard, my friend," says the other. "I'm a man of few words, blunt and honest. If you have anything to say, be plain. Don't think I can be losing my time with such a pitiful rascal as you are."

"Well," says Bill. "I want money, then, and am ready to come into terms. What have you to say to that, Nick?"

"Let me see—let me look at you," says his companion, turning him about. "Now, Bill, in the first place, are you not as finished a scarecrow as ever stood upon two legs?"

"I play second fiddle to you there again," says Bill.

"There you stand, with the blackguards' coat of arms quartered under your eye, and—"

"Don't make little of *black*guards," said Bill, "nor spake disparagingly of your *own* crest."

"Why, what would you bring, you brazen rascal, if you were fairly put up at auction?"

"Faith, I'd bring more bidders than you would," said Bill, "if you were to go off at auction tomorrow. I tell you they should bid *downward* to come to your value, Nicholas. We have no coin *small* enough to purchase you."

"Well, no matter," said Nick. "If you are willing to be mine at the expiration of seven years, I will give you more money than ever the rascally breed of you was worth."

"Done!" said Bill. "But no disparagement to my family, in the meantime; so down with the hard cash, and don't be a *neger*."

The money was accordingly paid down; but as nobody was present, except the giver and receiver, the amount of what Bill got was never known.

"Won't you give me a luck penny?" said the old gentleman.

"Tut," said Billy, "so prosperous an old fellow as you cannot want it; however, bad luck to you, with all my heart! and it's rubbing grease to a fat pig to say so. Be off now, or I'll commit suicide on you. Your absence is a cordial to most people, you infernal old profligate. You have injured my morals even for the short time you have been with me, for I don't find myself so virtuous as I was."

"Is that your gratitude, Billy?"

"Is it gratitude *you* speak of, man? I wonder you don't blush when you name it. However, when you come again, if you bring a third eye in your head you will see what I mane, Nicholas, *ahagur*."

The old gentleman, as Bill spoke, hopped across the ditch on his way to *Downing* Street, where of late 'tis thought he possesses much influence.

Bill now began by degrees to show off, but still wrought a little at his trade to blindfold the neighbors. In a very short time, however, he became a great man. So long indeed as he was a poor rascal, no decent person would speak to him; even the proud servingmen at the "Big House" would turn up their noses at him. And he well deserved to be made little of by others, because he was mean enough to make little of himself. But when it was seen and known that he had oceans of money, it was wonderful to think, although he was *now* a greater blackguard than ever, how those who despised him before began to come round him and court his company. Bill, however, had neither sense nor spirit to make those sunshiny friends know their distance; not he—instead of that he was proud to be seen in decent company, and so long as the money lasted, it was "hail fellow well met" between himself and every fair-faced *spunger* who had a horse under him, a decent coat to his back, and a good appetite to eat his dinners. With riches and all, Bill was the same man still; but, somehow or other, there is a great difference between a rich profligate and a poor one, and Bill found it so to his cost in *both* cases.

Before half the seven years was passed, Bill had his carriage and his equipages; was hand and glove with my Lord This, and my Lord That; kept hounds and hunters; was the first sportsman at the Curragh; patronized every boxing ruffian he could pick up; and betted night and day on cards, dice, and horses. Bill, in short, *should* be a blood, and except he did all this, he could not presume to mingle with the fashionable bloods of his time.

It's an old proverb, however, that "what is got over the Devil's back is sure to go off under it," and in Bill's case this proved true. In short, the old boy himself could not supply him with money so fast as he made it fly; it was "come easy, go easy," with Bill, and so sign was on it, before he came within two years of his time he found his purse empty.

And now came the value of his summer friends to be known. When it was discovered that the cash was no longer flush with him—that stud, and carriage, and hounds were going to the hammer—whish! off they went, friends, relations, pot companions, dinner eaters, black-legs, and all, like a flock of crows that had smelled gunpowder. Down Bill soon went, week after week and day after day, until at last he was obliged to put on the leather apron and take to the hammer again; and not only that, for as no experience could make him wise, he once more began his taproom brawls, his quarrels with Judy, and took to his "high feeding" at the dry potatoes and salt. Now, too, came the cutting tongues of all who knew him, like razors upon him. Those that he scorned because they were poor and himself rich now paid him back his own with interest; and those that he had measured himself with, because they were rich, and who only countenanced him in consequence of his wealth, gave him the hardest word in their cheeks. The Devil mend him! He deserved it all, and more if he had got it.

Bill, however, who was a hardened sinner, never fretted himself down an ounce of flesh by what was said to him or of him. Not he; he cursed, and fought, and swore, and schemed away as usual, taking in everyone he could; and surely none could match him at villainy of all sorts and sizes.

At last the seven years became expired, and Bill was one morning sitting in his forge, sober and hungry, the wife cursing him, and the children squalling as before; he was thinking how he might defraud some honest neighbor out of a breakfast to stop their mouths and his own, too, when who walks in to him but old Nick to demand his bargain.

"Morrow, Bill!" says he with a sneer.

"The Devil welcome you!" says Bill. "But you have a fresh memory."

"A bargain's a bargain between two *honest* men, any day," says Satan; "when I speak of honest men, I mean yourself and *me*, Bill"; and he put his tongue in his cheek to make game of the unfortunate rogue he had come for.

"Nick, my worthy fellow," said Bill, "have bowels; you wouldn't do a shabby thing; you wouldn't disgrace your own character by putting more weight upon a falling man. You know what it is to get a *comedown* yourself, my worthy; so just keep your toe in your pump, and walk off with yourself somewhere else. A *cool* walk will sarve you better than my company, Nicholas."

"Bill, it's no use in shirking," said his friend; "your swindling tricks may enable you to cheat others, but you won't cheat *me*, I guess. You want nothing to make you perfect in your way but to travel; and travel you shall under my guidance, Billy. No, no—I'm not to be swindled, my good fellow. I have rather a—a—better opinion of myself, Mr. D., than to think that you could outwit one Nicholas Clutie, Esq.—ahem!"

"You may sneer, you sinner," replied Bill, "but I tell you that I have outwitted men who could buy and sell you to your face. Despair, you villain, when I tell you that *no attorney* could stand before me."

Satan's countenance got blank when he heard this; he wriggled and fidgeted about and appeared to be not quite comfortable.

"In that case, then," says he, "the sooner I *deceive* you the better; so turn out for the *Low Countries*."

"Is it come to that in earnest?" said Bill. "And are you going to act the rascal at the long run?"

"'Pon honor, Bill."

"Have patience, then, you sinner, till I finish this horseshoe—it's the last of a set I'm finishing for one of your friend the attorney's horses. And here, Nick, I hate idleness; you know it's the mother of mischief; take this sledge hammer and give a dozen strokes or so, till I get it out of hands, and then here's with you, since it must be so."

He then gave the bellows a puff that blew half a peck of dust in Clubfoot's face, whipped out the red-hot iron, and set Satan sledging away for bare life.

"Faith," says Bill to him, when the shoe was finished, "it's a thousand pities ever the sledge should be out of your hand; the great *Parra Gow* was a child to you at sledging, you're such an able tyke. Now just exercise yourself till I bid the wife and *childhre* good-by, and then I'm off."

Out went Bill, of course, without the slightest notion of coming back; no more than Nick had that he could not give up the sledging, and indeed neither could he, but was forced to work away as if he was sledging for a wager. This was just what Bill wanted. He was now compelled to sledge on until it was Bill's pleasure to release him; and so we leave him very industriously employed, while we look after the worthy who outwitted him.

In the meantime Bill broke cover and took to the country at large; wrought a little journey work wherever he could get it, and in this way went from one place to another, till, in the course of a month, he walked back very coolly into his own forge to see how things went on in his absence. There he found Satan in a rage, the perspiration pouring from him in torrents, hammering with might and main upon the naked anvil. Bill calmly leaned back against the wall, placed his hat upon the side of his head, put his hands into his breeches pockets, and began to whistle *Shaun Gow's* hornpipe. At length he says, in a very quiet and good-humored way:

"Morrow, Nick!"

"Oh!" says Nick, still hammering away. "Oh! you double-distilled villain (hech!), may the most refined ornamental (hech!) collection of curses that ever was gathered (hech!) into a single nosegay of ill fortune (hech!) shine in the buttonhole of your conscience (hech!) while your name is Bill Dawson! I denounce you (hech!) as a doublemilled villain, a finished, hot-pressed knave (hech!), in comparison of whom all the other knaves I ever knew (hech!), attorneys included, are honest men. I brand you (hech!) as the pearl of cheats, a tiptop take-in (hech!). I denounce you, I say again, for the villainous treatment (hech!) I have received at your hands in this most untoward (hech!) and unfortunate transaction between us; for (hech!) unfortunate, in every sense, is he that has anything to do with (hech!) such a prime and finished impostor."

"You're very warm, Nicky," says Bill; "what puts you into a passion, you old sinner? Sure if it's your own will and pleasure to take exercise at my anvil, *I'm* not to be abused for it. Upon my credit, Nicky, you ought to blush for using such blackguard language, so unbecoming your grave character. You cannot say that it was I set you a-hammering at the empty anvil, you profligate.

"However, as you are so very industrious, I simply say it would be a thousand pities to take you from it. Nick, I love industry in my heart, and I always encourage it, so work away; it's not often you spend your time so creditably. I'm afraid if you weren't at that you'd be worse employed."

"Bill, have bowels," said the operative; "you wouldn't go to lay more weight on a falling man, you know; you wouldn't disgrace your character by such a piece of iniquity as keeping an inoffensive gentleman advanced in years, at such an unbecoming and rascally job as this. Generosity's your top virtue, Bill; not but that you have many other excellent ones, as well as that, among which, as you say yourself, I reckon industry; but still it is in generosity you shine. Come, Bill, honor bright, and release me."

"Name the terms, you profligate."

"You're above terms, William; a generous fellow like you never thinks of terms."

"Good-by, old gentleman!" said Bill very coolly. "I'll drop in to see you once a month."

"No, no, Bill, you infern—a—a—. You excellent, worthy, delightful fellow, not so fast; not so fast. Come, name your terms, you sland—My dear Bill, name your terms."

"Seven years more."

"I agree; but—"

"And the same supply of cash as before, down on the nail here."

"Very good; very good. You're rather simple, Bill; rather soft, I must confess. Well, no matter. I shall yet turn the tab—a—hem! You are an exceedingly simple fellow, Bill; still there will come a day, my *dear* Bill—there will come—'

"Do you grumble, you vagrant? Another word, and I double the terms."

"Mum, William—mum; *tace* is Latin for a candle."

"Seven years more of grace, and the same measure of the needful that I got before. Ay or no?"

"Of grace, Bill! Ay! Ay! Ay! There's the cash. I accept the terms. Oh, blood! The rascal—of grace! Bill!"

"Well, now drop the hammer and vanish," says Billy; "but what would you think to take this sledge, while you stay, and give me a—Eh! Why in such a hurry?" he added, seeing that

Satan withdrew in double-quick time.

"Hello! Nicholas!" he shouted. "Come back; you forgot something!" And when the old gentleman looked behind him, Billy shook the hammer at him, on which he vanished altogether.

Billy now got into his old courses; and what shows the kind of people the world is made of, he also took up with his old company. When they saw that he had the money once more and was sowing it about him in all directions, they immediately began to find excuses for his former extravagance.

"Say what you will," said one, "Bill Dawson's a spirited fellow that bleeds like a prince."

"He's a hospitable man in his own house, or out of it, as ever lived," said another.

"His only fault is," observed a third, "that he is, if anything, too generous and doesn't know the value of money; his fault's on the right side, however."

"He has the spunk in him," said a fourth; "keeps a capital table, prime wines, and a standing welcome for his friends."

"Why," said a fifth, "if he doesn't enjoy his money while he lives, he won't when he's dead; so more power to him, and a wider throat to his purse."

Indeed, the very persons who were cramming themselves at his expense despised him at heart. They knew very well, however, how to take him on the weak side. Praise his generosity, and he would do anything; call him a man of spirit, and you might fleece him to his face. Sometimes he would toss a purse of guineas to this knave, another to that flatterer, a third to a bully, and a fourth to some broken-down rake—and all to convince them that he was a sterling friend—a man of mettle and liberality. But never was he known to help a virtuous and struggling family—to assist the widow or the fatherless, or to do any other act that was truly useful. It is to be supposed the reason of this was that as he spent it, as most of the world do, in the service of the Devil, by whose aid he got it, he was prevented from turning it to a good account. Between you and me, dear reader, there are more persons acting after Bill's fashion in the same world than you dream about.

When his money was out again, his friends played him the same rascally game once more. No sooner did his poverty become plain than the knaves began to be troubled with small fits of modesty, such as an unwillingness to come to his place when there was no longer anything to be got there. A kind of virgin bashfulness prevented them from speaking to him when they saw him getting out on the wrong side of his clothes. Many of them would turn away from him in the prettiest and most delicate manner when they thought he wanted to borrow money from them—all for fear of putting him to the blush for asking it. Others again, when they saw him coming toward their houses about dinner hour, would become so confused, from mere gratitude, as to think themselves in another place; and their servants, seized, as it were, with the same feeling, would tell Bill that their masters were "not at home."

At length, after traveling the same villainous round as before, Bill was compelled to betake himself, as the last remedy, to the forge; in other words, he found that there is, after all, nothing in this world that a man can rely on so firmly and surely as his own industry. Bill, however, wanted the organ of common sense, for his experience—and it was sharp enough to leave an impression—ran off him like water off a duck.

He took to his employment sorely against his grain, but he had now no choice. He must either work or starve, and starvation is like a great doctor—nobody tries it till every other remedy fails them. Bill had been twice rich; twice a gentleman among blackguards, but always a blackguard among gentlemen, for no wealth or acquaintance with decent society could rub the rust of his native vulgarity off him. He was now a common blinking sot in his forge; a drunken bully in the taproom, cursing and browbeating everyone as well as his wife; boasting of how much money he had spent in his day; swaggering about the high doings he carried on; telling stories about himself and Lord This at the Curragh; the dinners he gave—how much they cost him—and attempting to extort credit upon the strength of his former wealth. He was too ignorant, however, to know that he was publishing his own disgrace and that it was a mean-spirited thing to be proud of what ought to make him blush through a deal board nine inches thick.

He was one morning industriously engaged in a quarrel with his wife, who, with a three-legged stool in her hand, appeared to mistake his head for his own anvil; he, in the meantime, paid his addresses to her with his leather apron, when who steps in to jog his memory about the little agreement that was between them but old Nick. The wife, it seems, in spite of all her exertions to the contrary, was getting the worst of it; and Sir Nicholas, willing to appear a gentleman of great gallantry, thought he could not do less than take up the lady's quarrel, particularly as Bill had laid her in a sleeping posture. Now Satan thought this too bad, and as he felt himself under many obligations to the sex, he determined to defend one of them on the present occasion; so as Judy rose, he turned upon her husband and floored him by a clever facer.

"You unmanly villain," said he, "is this the way you treat your wife? 'Pon honor Bill, I'll chastise you on the spot. I could not stand by, a spectator of such ungentlemanly conduct, without giving you all claim to gallant—" Whack! The word was divided in his mouth by the blow of a churnstaff from Judy, who no sooner saw Bill struck than she nailed Satan, who "fell" once more.

"What, you villain! That's for striking my husband like a murderer behind his back," said Judy, and she suited the action to the word. "That's for interfering between man and wife. Would you murder the poor man before my face, eh? If he bates me, you shabby dog you, who has a better right? I'm sure it's nothing out of your pocket. Must you have your finger in every pie?"

This was anything but *idle* talk, for at every word she gave him a remembrance, hot and heavy. Nicholas backed, danced, and hopped; she advanced, still drubbing him with great perseverance, till at length he fell into the redoubtable armchair, which stood exactly behind him. Bill, who had been putting in two blows for Judy's one, seeing that his enemy was safe, now got between the Devil and his wife, *a situation that few will be disposed to envy him.*

"Tenderness, Judy," said the husband; "I hate cruelty. Go put the tongs in the fire, and make them red-hot. Nicholas, you have a nose," said he.

Satan began to rise but was rather surprised to find that he could not budge.

"Nicholas," says Bill, "how is your pulse? You don't look well; that is to say, you look worse than usual."

The other attempted to rise but found it a mistake.

"I'll thank you to come along," said Bill. "I have a fancy to travel under your guidance, and we'll take the *Low Countries* in our way, won't we? Get to your legs, you sinner; you know a bargain's a bargain between two *honest* men, Nicholas, meaning *yourself* and *me*. Judy, are the tongs hot?"

Satan's face was worth looking at as he turned his eyes from the husband to the wife and then fastened them on the tongs, now nearly at a furnace heat in the fire, conscious at the same time that he could not move out of the chair.

"Billy," said he, "you won't forget that I rewarded you generously the last time I saw you, in the way of business."

"Faith, Nicholas, it fails me to remember any generosity I ever showed you. Don't be womanish. I simply want to see what kind of stuff your nose is made of and whether it will stretch like a rogue's conscience. If it does we will flatter it up the chimly with red-hot tongs, and when this old hat is fixed on the top of it, let us alone for a weathercock."

"Have a *fellow feeling*, Mr. Dawson; you know we ought not to dispute. Drop the matter, and I give you the next seven years."

"We know all that," says Billy, opening the red-hot tongs very coolly.

"Mr. Dawson," said Satan, "if you cannot remember my friendship to yourself, don't forget how often I stood your father's friend, your grandfather's friend, and the friend of all your relations up to the tenth generation. I intended, also, to stand by your children after you, so long as the name of Dawson—and a respectable one it is—might last."

"Don't be blushing, Nick," says Bill; "you are too modest; that was ever your failing; hold up your head, there's money bid for you. I'll give you such a nose, my good friend, that you will have to keep an outrider before you, to carry the end of it on his shoulder."

"Mr. Dawson, I pledge my honor to raise your children in the world as high as they can go, no matter whether they desire it or not."

"That's very kind of you," says the other, "and I'll do as much for your nose."

He gripped it as he spoke, and the old boy immediately sung

out; Bill pulled, and the nose went with him like a piece of warm wax. He then transferred the tongs to Judy, got a ladder, resumed the tongs, ascended the chimney, and tugged stoutly at the nose until he got it five feet above the roof. He then fixed the hat upon the top of it and came down.

"There's a weathercock," said Billy; "I defy Ireland to show such a beauty. Faith, Nick, it would make the purtiest steeple for a church in all Europe, and the old hat fits it to a shaving."

In this state, with his nose twisted up the chimney, Satan sat for some time, experiencing the novelty of what might be termed a peculiar sensation. At last the worthy husband and wife began to relent.

"I think," said Bill, "that we have made the most of the nose, as well as the joke; I believe, Judy, it's long enough."

"What is?" says Judy.

"Why, the joke," said the husband.

"Faith, and I think so is the nose," said Judy.

"What do you say yourself, Satan?" said Bill.

"Nothing at all, William," said the other; "but that—ha! ha!—it's a good joke—an excellent joke, and a goodly nose, too, as it *stands*. You were always a gentlemanly man, Bill, and did things with a grace; still, if I might give an opinion on such a trifle—"

"It's no trifle at all," says Bill, "if you spake of the nose."

"Very well, it is not," says the other; "still, I am decidedly of opinion that if you could shorten both the joke and the nose without further violence, you would lay me under very heavy obligations, which I shall be ready to acknowledge and *repay* as I ought."

"Come," said Bill, "shell out once more, and be off for seven years. As much as you came down with the last time, and vanish."

The words were scarcely spoken, when the money was at his feet and Satan invisible. Nothing could surpass the mirth of Bill and his wife at the result of this adventure. They laughed till they fell down on the floor.

It is useless to go over the same ground again. Bill was still incorrigible. The money went as the Devil's money always goes. Bill caroused and squandered but could never turn a penny of it to a good purpose. In this way year after year went, till the seventh was closed and Bill's hour come. He was now, and had been for some time past, as miserable a knave as ever. Not a shilling had he, nor a shilling's worth, with the exception of his forge, his cabin, and a few articles of crazy furniture. In this state he was standing in his forge as before, straining his ingenuity how to make out a breakfast, when Satan came to look after him. The old gentleman was sorely puzzled how to get at him. He kept skulking and sneaking about the forge for some time, till he saw that Bill hadn't a cross to bless himself with. He immediately changed himself into a guinea and lay in an open place where he knew Bill would see him. "If," said he, "I once get into his possession, I can manage him." The honest smith took the bait, for it was well gilded; he clutched the guinea, put it into his purse, and closed it up. "Ho! Ho!" shouted the Devil out of the purse. "You're caught, Bill; I've secured you at last, you knave you. Why don't you despair you villain, when you think of what's before you?"

"Why, you unlucky ould dog," said Bill, "is it there you are? Will you always drive your head into every loophole that's set for you? Faith, Nick *achora,* I never had you bagged till now."

Satan then began to tug and struggle with a view of getting out of the purse, but in vain.

"Mr. Dawson," said he, "we understand each other. I'll give the seven years additional and the cash on the nail."

"Be aisey, Nicholas. You know the weight of the hammer, that's enough. It's not a whipping with feathers you're going to get, anyhow. Just be aisey."

"Mr. Dawson, I grant I'm not your match. Release me, and I double the case. I was merely trying your temper when I took the shape of a guinea."

"Faith and I'll try yours before I lave it, I've a notion." He immediately commenced with the sledge, and Satan sang out with a considerable want of firmness. "Am I heavy enough?" said Bill.

"Lighter, lighter, William, if you love me. I haven't been well latterly, Mr. Dawson—I have been delicate—my health, in short, is in a very precarious state, Mr. Dawson."

"I can believe *that*,' said Bill, "and it will be more so before I have done with you. Am I doing it right?"

"Bill," said Nick, "is this gentlemanly treatment in your own respectable shop? Do you think, if you dropped into my little place, that I'd act this rascally part toward you? Have you no compunction?"

"I know," replied Bill, sledging away with vehemence, "that you're notorious for giving your friends a *warm* welcome. Divil an ould youth more so; but you must be daling in bad coin, must you? However, good or bad, you're in for a sweat now, you sinner. Am I doin' it purty?"

"Lovely, William—but, if possible, a little more delicate."

"Oh, how delicate you are! Maybe a cup o' tay would sarve you, or a little small gruel to compose your stomach?"

"Mr. Dawson," said the gentleman in the purse, "hold your hand and let us understand one another. I have a proposal to make."

"Hear the sinner anyhow," said the wife.

"Name your own sum," said Satan, "only set me free."

"No, the sorra may take the toe you'll budge till you let Bill off," said the wife; "hould him hard, Bill, barrin' he sets you clear of your engagement."

"There it is, my posy," said Bill; "that's the condition. If you don't give *me up*, here's at you once more—and you must double the cash you gave the last time, too. So, if you're of that opinion, say *ay*—leave the cash and be off."

The money appeared in a glittering heap before Bill, upon which he exclaimed, "The *ay* has it, you dog. Take to your pumps now, and fair weather after you, you vagrant; but, Nicholas—Nick—here, here—" The other looked back and saw Bill, with a broad grin upon him, shaking the purse at him. "Nicholas, come back," said he. "I'm short a guinea." Nick shook his fist and disappeared.

It would be useless to stop now, merely to inform our readers that Bill was beyond improvement. In short, he once more took to his old habits and lived on exactly in the same manner as before. He had two sons—one as great a blackguard as himself, and who was also named after him; the other was a well-conducted, virtuous young man called James, who left his father and, having relied upon his own industry and honest perseverance in life, arrived afterward to great wealth and built the town called Castle Dawson, which is so called from its founder until this day.

Bill, at length, in spite of all his wealth, was obliged, as he himself said, "to travel"—in other words, he fell asleep one day and forgot to awaken; or, in still plainer terms, he died.

Now, it is usual, when a man dies, to close the history of his life and adventures at once; but with our hero this cannot be the case. The moment Bill departed he very naturally bent his steps toward the residence of St. Moroky, as being, in his opinion, likely to lead him toward the snuggest berth he could readily make out. On arriving, he gave a very humble kind of knock, and St. Moroky appeared.

"God save your Reverence!" said Bill, very submissively.

"Be off; there's no admittance here for so poor a youth as you are," said St. Moroky.

He was now so cold and fatigued that he cared like where he went, provided only, as he said himself, "he could rest his bones and get an air of the fire." Accordingly, after arriving at a large black gate, he knocked, as before, and was told he would get *instant* admittance the moment he gave his name.

"Billy Dawson," he replied.

"Off, instantly," said the porter to his companions, "and let His Majesty know that the rascal he dreads so much is here at the gate."

Such a racket and tumult were never heard as the very mention of Billy Dawson created.

In the meantime, his old acquaintance came running toward the gate with such haste and consternation that his tail was several times nearly tripping up his heels.

"Don't admit that rascal," he shouted; "bar the gate—make every chain and lock and bolt fast—I won't be safe—and I won't stay here, nor none of us need stay here, if he gets in—my bones are sore yet after him. No, no—begone, you villain—you'll get no entrance here—I know you too well."

Bill could not help giving a broad, malicious grin at Satan, and, putting his nose through the bars, he exclaimed, "Ha! You ould dog, I have you afraid of me at last, have I?"

He had scarcely uttered the words, when his foe, who stood inside, instantly tweaked him by the nose, and Bill felt as if he had been gripped by the same red-hot tongs with which he himself had formerly tweaked the nose of Nicholas.

Bill then departed but soon found that in consequence of the inflammable materials which strong drink had thrown into his nose, that organ immediately took fire, and, indeed, to tell the truth, kept burning night and day, winter and summer, without ever once going out from that hour to this.

Such was the sad fate of Billy Dawson, who has been walking without stop or stay, from place to place, ever since; and in consequence of the flame on his nose, and his beard being tangled like a wisp of hay, he has been christened by the country folk Will-O'-the-Wisp, while, as it were, to show the mischief of his disposition, the circulating knave, knowing that he must seek the coldest bogs and quagmires in order to cool his nose, seizes upon that opportunity of misleading the unthinking and tipsy night travelers from their way, just that he may have the satisfaction of still taking in as many as possible.

Hertford O'Donnell's Warning
Charlotte Riddell

MANY A YEAR, before chloroform was thought of, there lived in an old rambling house, in Gerrard Street, Soho, a clever Irishman called Hertford O'Donnell.

After Hertford O'Donnell he was entitled to write, MRCS for he had studied hard to gain this distinction, and the older surgeons at Guy's (his hospital) considered him one of the most rising operators of the day.

Having said chloroform was unknown at the time this story opens, it will strike my readers that, if Hertford O'Donnell were a rising and successful operator in those days, of necessity he combined within himself a larger number of striking qualities than are by any means necessary to form a successful operator in these.

There was more than mere hand skill, more than even thorough knowledge of his profession, then needful for the man, who, dealing with conscious subjects, essayed to rid them of some of the diseases to which flesh is heir. There was greater courage required in the manipulator of old than is altogether essential at present. Then, as now, a thorough mastery of his instruments, a steady hand, a keen eye, a quick dexterity were indispensable to a good operator; but, added to all these things, there formerly required a pulse which knew no quickening, a mental strength which never faltered, a ready power of adaptation in unexpected circumstances, fertility of resource in difficult cases, and a brave front under all emergencies.

If I refrain from adding that a hard as well as a courageous heart was an important item in the program, it is only out of deference to general opinion, which, among other strange delusions, clings to the belief that courage and hardness are antagonistic qualities.

Hertford O'Donnell, however, was hard as steel. He understood his work, and he did it thoroughly; but he cared no more for quivering nerves and shrinking muscles, for screams of agony, for faces white with pain, and teeth clenched in the extremity of anguish, than he did for the stony countenances of the dead, which so often in the dissecting room appalled younger and less experienced men.

He had no sentiment, and he had no sympathy. The human body was to him merely an ingenious piece of mechanism, which it was at once a pleasure and a profit to understand. Precisely as Brunel loved the Thames Tunnel, or any other singular engineering feat, so O'Donnell loved a patient on whom he had operated successfully, more especially if the ailment possessed by the patient were of a rare and difficult character.

And for this reason he was much liked by all who came under his hands, since patients are apt to mistake a surgeon's interest in their cases for interest in themselves; and it was gratifying to John Dicks, plasterer, and Timothy Regan, laborer, to be the happy possessors of remarkable diseases, which produced a cordial understanding between them and the handsome Irishman.

If he had been hard and cool at the moment of hacking them to pieces, that was all forgotten or remembered only as a virtue, when, after being discharged from hospital like soldiers who have served in a severe campaign, they met Mr. O'Donnell in the street, and were accosted by that rising individual just as though he considered himself nobody.

He had a royal memory, this stranger in a strange land, both for faces and cases; and like the rest of his countrymen, he never felt it beneath his dignity to talk cordially to corduroy and fustian.

In London, as at Calgillan, he never held back his tongue from speaking a cheery or a kindly word. His manners were pliable enough, if his heart were not; and the porters, and the patients, and the nurses, and the students at Guy's were all pleased to see Hertford O'Donnell.

Rain, hail, sunshine, it was all the same; there was a life and a brightness about the man which communicated itself to those with whom he came in contact. Let the mud in the Borough be a foot deep or the London fog as thick as peasoup, Mr. O'Donnell never lost his temper, never muttered a surly reply to the gatekeeper's salutation, but spoke out blithely and cheerfully to his pupils and his patients, to the sick and to the well, to those below and to those above him.

And yet, spite of all these good qualities, spite of his

handsome face, his fine figure, his easy address, and his unquestionable skill as an operator, the dons, who acknowledged his talent, shook their heads gravely when two or three of them in private and solemn conclave talked confidentially of their younger brother.

If there were many things in his favor, there were more in his disfavor. He was Irish—not merely by the accident of birth, which might have been forgiven, since a man cannot be held accountable for such caprices of Nature, but by every other accident and design which is objectionable to the orthodox and respectable and representative English mind.

In speech, appearance, manner, taste, modes of expression, habits of life, Hertford O'Donnell was Irish. To the core of his heart he loved the island which he declared he never meant to re-visit; and among the English he moved to all intents and purposes a foreigner, who was resolved, so said the great prophets at Guy's, to rush to destruction as fast as he could, and let no man hinder him.

"He means to go the whole length of his tether," observed one of the ancient wiseacres to another; which speech implied a conviction that Hertford O'Donnell, having sold himself to the Evil One, had determined to dive the full length of his rope into wickedness before being pulled to that shore where even wickedness is negative—where there are no mad carouses, no wild, sinful excitements, nothing but impotent wailing and gnashing of teeth.

A reckless, graceless, clever, wicked devil—going to his natural home as fast as in London anyone possibly speeds thither; this was the opinion his superiors held of the man who lived all alone with a housekeeper and her husband (who acted as butler) in his big house near Soho.

Gerrard Street—made famous by De Quincey—was not then

an utterly shady and forgotten locality; carriage-patients found their way to the rising young surgeon—some great personages thought it not beneath them to fee an individual whose consulting rooms were situated on what was even then considered the wrong side of Regent Street. He was making money, and he was spending it; he was over head and ears in debt—useless, vulgar debt—senselessly contracted, never bravely faced. He had lived at an awful pace ever since he came to London, a pace which only a man who hopes and expects to die young can ever travel.

Life was good, was it? Death, was he a child, or a woman, or a coward, to be afraid of that hereafter? God knew all about the trifle which had upset his coach, better than the dons at Guy's.

Hertford O'Donnell understood the world pretty thoroughly, and the ways thereof were to him as roads often traversed; therefore, when he said that at the Day of Judgment he felt certain he should come off as well as many of those who censured him, it may be assumed, that, although his views of post-mortem punishment were vague, unsatisfactory and infidel, still his information as to the peccadilloes of his neighbors was such as consoled himself.

And yet, living all alone in the old house near Soho Square, grave thoughts would intrude into the surgeon's mind—thoughts which were, so to say, italicized by peremptory letters, and still more peremptory visits from people who wanted money.

Although he had many acquaintances he had no single friend, and accordingly these thoughts were received and brooded over in solitude—in those hours when, after returning from dinner, or supper, or congenial carouse, he sat in his dreary rooms, smoking his pipe and considering means and ways, chances and certainties.

In good truth he had started in London with some vague idea that as his life in it would not be of long continuance, the pace at which he elected to travel could be of little consequence; but the years since his first entry into the Metropolis were now piled one on the top of another, his youth was behind him, his chances of longevity, spite of the way he had striven to injure his constitution, quite as good as ever. He had come to that period in existence, to that narrow strip of tableland, whence the ascent of youth and the descent of age are equally discernible—when, simply because he has lived for so many years, it strikes a man as possible he may have to live for just as many more, with the ability for hard work gone, with the boon companions scattered, with the capacity for enjoying convivial meetings a mere memory, with small means perhaps, with no bright hopes, with the pomp and the circumstance and the fairy carriages, and the glamor which youth flings over earthly objects, faded away like the pageant of yesterday, while the dreary ceremony of living has to be gone through today and tomorrow and the morrow after, as though the gay cavalcade and the martial music, and the glittering helmets and the prancing steeds were still accompanying the wayfarer to his journey's end.

Ah! my friends, there comes a moment when we must all leave the coach, with its four bright bays, its pleasant outside freight, its cheery company, its guard who blows the horn so merrily through villages and along lonely country roads.

Long before we reach that final stage, where the black business claims us for its own special property, we have to bid goodbye to all easy, thoughtless journeying, and betake ourselves, with what zest we may, to traversing the common of reality. There is no royal road across it that ever I heard of. From the king on his throne to the laborer who vaguely imagines what manner of being a king is, we have all to tramp across that desert at one period of our lives, at all events; and that period usually is when, as I have said, a man starts to find the hopes, and the strength, and the buoyancy of youth left behind, while years and years of life lie stretching out before him.

The coach he has traveled by drops him here. There is no appeal, there is no help; therefore, let him take off his hat and wish the new passengers good speed, without either envy or repining.

Behold, he has had his turn, and let whosoever will mount on the box-seat of life again, and tip the coachman and handle the ribbons—he shall take that pleasant journey no more, no more forever.

Even supposing a man's springtime to have been a cold and ungenial one, with bitter easterly winds and nipping frosts biting the buds and retarding the blossoms, still it was spring for all that—spring with the young green leaves sprouting forth, with the flowers unfolding tenderly, with the songs of the birds and the rush of waters, with the summer before and the autumn afar off, and winter remote as death and eternity, but when once the trees have donned their summer foliage, when the pure white blossoms have disappeared, and the gorgeous red and orange and purple blaze of many-colored flowers fills the gardens, then if there come a wet, dreary day, the idea of autumn and winter is not so difficult to realize. When once twelve o'clock is reached, the evening and night become facts, not possibilities; and it was of the afternoon, and the evening, and the night, Hertford O'Donnell sat thinking on the Christmas Eve, when I crave permission to introduce him to my readers.

A good-looking man ladies considered him. A tall, dark-complexioned, black-haired, straight-limbed, deeply divinely blue-eyed fellow, with a soft voice, with a pleasant brogue, who had ridden like a centaur over the loose stone walls in Connemara, who had danced all night at the Dublin balls, who had walked across the Bennebeola Mountains, gun in hand, day after day, without weariness, who had fished in every one of the hundred lakes you can behold from the top of that mountain near the Recess Hotel, who had led a mad, wild life in Trinity College, and a wilder, perhaps, while "studying for a doctor"— as the Irish phrase goes—in Edinburgh, and who, after the death of his eldest brother left him free to return to Calgillan, and pursue the usual utterly useless, utterly purposeless, utterly pleasant life of an Irish gentleman possessed of health, birth, and expectations, suddenly kicked over the paternal traces, bade adieu to Calgillan Castle and the blandishments of a certain beautiful Miss Clifden, beloved of his mother, and laid out to be his wife, walked down the avenue without even so much company as a gossoon to carry his carpet-bag, shook the dust from his feet at the lodge gates, and took his seat on the coach, never once looking back at Calgillan, where his favorite mare was standing in the stable, his greyhounds chasing one another round the home paddock, his gun at half-cock in his dressing-room and his fishing-tackle all in order and ready for use.

He had not kissed his mother, or asked for his father's blessing; he left Miss Clifden, arrayed in her brand-new riding-habit, without a word of affection or regret; he had spoken no syllable of farewell to any servant about the place; only when the old woman at the lodge bade him good morning and God-blessed his handsome face, he recommended her bitterly to look at it well for she would never see it more.

Twelve years and a half had passed since then, without either Miss Clifden or any other one of the Calgillan people having set eyes on Master Hertford's handsome face.

He had kept his vow to himself; he had not written home; he had not been indebted to mother or father for even a tenpenny-piece during the whole of that time; he had lived without friends; and he had lived without God—so far as God ever lets a man live without him.

One thing only he felt to be needful—money; money to keep him when the evil days of sickness, or age, or loss of practice came upon him. Though a spendthrift, he was not a simpleton; around him he saw men, who, having started with fairer prospects than his own, were, nevertheless, reduced to indigence; and he knew that what had happened to others might happen to himself.

An unlucky cut, slipping on a piece of orange-peel in the street, the merest accident imaginable, is sufficient to change opulence to beggary in the life's program of an individual, whose income depends on eye, on nerve, on hand; and, besides the consciousness of this fact, Hertford O'Donnell knew that beyond a certain point in his profession, progress was not easy.

It did not depend quite on the strength of his own bow and shield whether he counted his earnings by hundreds or thousands. Work may achieve competence; but mere work cannot, in a profession, at all events, compass fortune.

He looked around him, and he perceived that the majority of great men—great and wealthy—had been indebted for their elevation, more to the accident of birth, patronage, connection, or marriage, than to personal ability.

Personal ability, no doubt, they possessed; but then, little Jones, who lived in Frith Street, and who could barely keep himself and his wife and family, had ability, too, only he lacked the concomitants of success.

He wanted something or someone to puff him into notoriety—a brother at Court—a lord's leg to mend—a rich wife to give him prestige in Society; and in his absence of this something or someone, he had grown grey-haired and fainthearted while laboring for a world which utterly despises its most obsequious servants.

"Clatter along the streets with a pair of fine horses, snub the middle classes, and drive over the commonalty—that is the way to compass wealth and popularity in England," said Hertford O'Donnell, bitterly; and as the man desired wealth and popularity, he sat before his fire, with a foot on each hob, and a short pipe in his mouth, considering how he might best obtain the means to clatter along the streets in his carriage, and splash plebeians with mud from his wheels like the best.

In Dublin he could, by means of his name and connection, have done well; but then he was not in Dublin, neither did he want to be. The bitterest memories of his life were inseparable from the very name of the Green Island, and he had no desire to return to it.

Besides, in Dublin, heiresses are not quite so plentiful as in London; and an heiress, Hertford O'Donnell had decided, would do more for him than years of steady work.

A rich wife could clear him of debt, introduce him to fashionable practice, afford him that measure of social respectability which a medical bachelor invariably lacks, deliver him from the loneliness of Gerrard Street, and the domination of Mr. and Mrs. Coles.

To most men, deliberately bartering away their independence for money seems so prosaic a business that they strive to gloss it over even to themselves, and to assign every reason for their choice, save that which is really the influencing one.

Not so, however, with Hertford O'Donnell. He sat beside the fire scoffing over his proposed bargain—thinking of the lady's age, her money bags, her desirable house in town, her seat in the country, her snobbishness, her folly.

"It could be a fitting ending," he sneered, "and why I did not settle the matter tonight passes my comprehension. I am not a fool, to be frightened with old women's tales; and yet I must have turned white. I felt I did, and she asked me whether I were ill. And then to think of my being such an idiot as to ask her if she had heard anything like a cry, as though she would be likely to hear that, she with her poor parvenu blood, which I often imagine must have been mixed with some of her father's strong pickling vinegar. What a deuce could I have been dreaming about? I wonder what it really was." And Hertford O'Donnell pushed his hair back off his forehead, and took another draught from the too familiar tumbler, which was placed conveniently on the chimney-piece.

"After expressly making up my mind to propose, too!" he mentally continued. "Could it have been conscience—that myth, which somebody, who knew nothing about the matter, said, 'Makes cowards of us all'? I don't believe in conscience; and even if there be such a thing capable of being developed by sentiment and cultivation, why should it trouble me? I have no intention of wronging Miss Janice Price Ingot, not the least. Honestly and fairly I shall marry her; honestly and fairly I shall act by her. An old wife is not exactly an ornamental article of furniture in a man's house; and I do not know that the fact of her being well gilded makes her look any handsomer. But she shall have no cause for complaint; and I will go and dine with her tomorrow, and settle the matter."

Having arrived at which resolution, Mr. O'Donnell arose, kicked down the fire—burning hollow—with the heel of his boot, knocked the ashes out of his pipe, emptied his tumbler, and bethought him it was time to go to bed. He was not in the habit of taking his rest so early as a quarter to twelve o'clock; but he felt unusually weary—tired mentally and bodily—and lonely beyond all power of expression.

"The fair Janet would be better than this," he said, half aloud;

and then, with a start and a shiver, and a blanched face, he turned sharply round, while a low, sobbing, wailing cry echoed mournfully through the room. No form of words could give an idea of the sound. The plaintiveness of the Aeolian harp—that plaintiveness which so soon affects and lowers the highest spirits—would have seemed wildly gay in comparison with the sadness of the cry which seemed floating in the air. As the summer wind comes and goes among the trees, so that mournful wail came and went—came and went. It came in a rush of sound, like a gradual crescendo managed by a skilful musician, and died away in a lingering note, so gently that the listener could scarcely tell the exact moment when it faded into utter silence.

I say faded, for it disappeared as the coastline disappears in the twilight, and there was total stillness in the apartment.

Then, for the first time, Hertford O'Donnell looked at his dog, and beholding the creature crouched into a corner beside the fireplace, called upon him to come out.

His voice sounded strange even to himself, and apparently the dog thought so too, for he made no effort to obey the summons.

"Come here, sir," his master repeated, and then the animal came crawling reluctantly forward with his hair on end, his eyes almost starting from his head, trembling violently, as the surgeon, who caressed him, felt.

"So you heard it, Brian?" he said to the dog. "And so your ears are sharper than Miss Ingot's, old fellow. It's a mighty queer thing to think of, being favored with a visit from a Banshee in Gerrard Street; and as the lady has traveled so far, I only wish I knew whether there is any sort of refreshment she would like to take after her long journey."

He spoke loudly, and with a certain mocking defiance, seeming to think the phantom he addressed would reply; but when he stopped at the end of his sentence, no sound came through the stillness. There was a dead silence in the room—a silence broken only by the falling of cinders on the hearth and the breathing of his dog.

"If my visitor would tell me," he proceeded, for whom this lamentation is being made, whether for myself, or for some member of my illustrious family, I should feel immensely obliged. It seems too much honor for a poor surgeon to have such attention paid him. Good Heavens! What is that?" he exclaimed, as a ring, loud and peremptory, woke all the echoes in the house, and brought his housekeeper, in a state of distressing dishabille, "out of her warm bed," as she subsequently stated, to the head of the staircase.

Across the hall Hertford O'Donnell strode, relieved at the prospect of speaking to any living being. He took no precaution of putting up the chain, but flung the door wide. A dozen burglars would have proved welcome in comparison with that ghostly intruder he had been interviewing; therefore, as has been said, he threw the door wide, admitting a rush of wet, cold air, which made poor Mrs. Coles' few remaining teeth chatter in her head.

"Who is there? What do you want?" asked the surgeon, seeing no person, and hearing no voice. "Who is there? Why the devil can't you speak?"

When even this polite exhortation failed to elicit an answer, he passed out into the night and looked up the street and down the street, to see nothing but the driving rain and the blinking lights.

"If this goes on much longer I shall soon think I must be either mad or drunk," he muttered, as he re-entered the house and locked and bolted the door once more.

"Lord's sake! What is the matter, sir?" asked Mrs. Coles,

from the upper flight, careful only to reveal the borders of her night-cap to Mr. O'Donnell's admiring gaze. "Is anybody killed? Have you to go out, sir?"

"It was only a runaway rig," he answered, trying to reassure himself with an explanation he did not in his heart believe.

"Runaway—I'd run away them!" murmured Mrs. Coles, as she retired to the conjugal couch, where Coles was, to quote her own expression, "snoring like a pig through it all."

Almost immediately afterwards she heard her master ascend the stairs and close his bedroom door.

"Madam will surely be too much of a gentlewoman to intrude here," thought the surgeon, scoffing even at his own fears; but when he lay down he did not put out his light, and made Brian leap up and crouch on the coverlet beside him.

The man was fairly frightened, and would have thought it no discredit to his manhood to acknowledge as much. He was not afraid of death, he was not afraid of trouble, he was not afraid of danger; but he was afraid of the Banshee; and as he lay with his hand on the dog's head, he recalled the many stories he had been told concerning this family retainer in the days of his youth.

He had not thought about her for years and years. Never before had he heard her voice himself. When his brother died she had not thought it necessary to travel up to Dublin and give him notice of the impending catastrophe. "If she had, I would have gone down to Calgillan, and perhaps saved his life,' considered the surgeon. "I wonder who this is for? If for me, that will settle my debts and my marriage. If I could be quite certain it was either of the old people, I would start tomorrow."

Then vaguely his mind wandered on to think of every Banshee story he had ever heard in his life. About the beautiful lady with the wreath of flowers, who sat on the rocks below Red

Castle, in the County Antrim, crying till one of the sons died for love of her; about the Round Chamber at Dunluce, which was swept clean by the Banshee every night; about the bed in a certain great house in Ireland, which was slept in constantly, although no human being ever passed in or out after dark; about that General Officer who, the night before Waterloo, said to a friend, "I have heard the Banshee, and shall not come off the field alive tomorrow; break the news gently to poor Carry"; and who, nevertheless, coming safe off the field, had subsequently news about poor Carry broken tenderly and pitifully to him; about the lad, who, aloft in the rigging, hearing through the night a sobbing and wailing coming over the waters, went down to the captain and told him he was afraid they were somehow out of their reckoning, just in time to save the ship, which, when morning broke, they found but for his warning would have been on the rocks. It was blowing great guns, and the sea was all in a fret and turmoil, and they could sometimes see in the trough of the waves, as down a valley, the cruel black reefs they had escaped.

On deck the captain stood speaking to the boy who had saved them, and asking how he knew of their danger; and when the lad told him, the captain laughed, and said her ladyship had been outwitted that time.

But the boy answered, with a grave shake of his head, that the warning was either for him or his, and that if he got safe to port there would be bad tidings waiting for him from home; whereupon the captain bade him go below, and get some brandy and lie down.

He got the brandy, and he lay down, but he never rose again; and when the storm abated—when a great calm succeeded to the previous tempest—there was a very solemn funeral at sea; and on their arrival at Liverpool the captain took a journey to

Ireland to tell a widowed mother how her only son died, and to bear his few effects to the poor desolate soul.

And Hertford O'Donnell thought again about his own father riding full-chase across country, and hearing, as he galloped by a clump of plantation, something like a sobbing and wailing. The hounds were in full cry, but he still felt, as he afterwards expressed it, that there was something among those trees he could not pass; and so he jumped off his horse, and hung the reins over the branch of a Scotch fir, and beat the cover well, but not a thing could he find in it.

Then, for the first time in his life, Miles O'Donnell turned his horse's head from the hunt, and, within a mile of Calgillan, met a man running to tell him his brother's gun had burst, and injured him mortally.

And he remembered the story also, of how Mary O'Donnell, his great aunt, being married to a young Englishman, heard the Banshee as she sat one evening waiting for his return; and of how she, thinking the bridge by which he often came home unsafe for horse and man, went out in a great panic, to meet and entreat him to go round by the main road for her sake. Sir Edward was riding along in the moonlight, making straight for the bridge, when he beheld a figure dressed all in white crossing it. Then there was a crash, and the figure disappeared.

The lady was rescued and brought back to the hall; but next morning there were two dead bodies within its walls—those of Lady Eyreton and her stillborn son.

Quicker than I write them, these memories chased one another through Hertford O'Donnell's brain; and there was one more terrible memory than any, which would recur to him, concerning an Irish nobleman who, seated alone in his great town house in London, heard the Banshee, and rushed out to get rid of the phantom, which wailed in his ear, nevertheless, as he strode down Piccadilly. And then the surgeon remembered how that nobleman went with a friend to the opera, feeling sure that there no Banshee, unless she had a box, could find admittance, until suddenly he heard her singing up among the highest part of the scenery, with a terrible mournfulness, and a pathos which made the prima donna's tenderest notes seem harsh by comparison.

As he came out, some quarrel arose between him and a famous fire-eater, against whom he stumbled; and the result was that the next afternoon there was a new Lord, for he was killed in a duel with Captain Bravo.

Memories like these are not the most enlivening possible; they are apt to make a man fanciful, and nervous, and wakeful; but as time ran on, Hertford O'Donnell fell asleep, with his candle still burning, and Brian's cold nose pressed against his hand.

He dreamt of his mother's family—the Hertfords of Artingbury, Yorkshire, far-off relatives of Lord Hertford—so far off that even Mrs. O'Donnell held no clue to the genealogical maze.

He thought he was at Artingbury, fishing; that it was a misty summer morning, and the fish rising beautifully. In his dreams he hooked one after another, and the boy who was with him threw them into the basket.

At last there was one more difficult to land than the others; and the boy, in his eagerness to watch the sport, drew nearer and nearer to the bnnk, while the fisher, intent on his prey, failed to notice his companion's danger.

Suddenly there was a cry, a splash, and the boy disappeared from sight.

Next instance he rose again, however, and then, for the first time, Hertford O'Donnell saw his face.

It was one he knew well.

In a moment he plunged into the water, and struck out for the lad. He had him by the hair, he was turning to bring him back to land, when the stream suddenly changed into a wide, wild, shoreless sea, where the billows were chasing one another with a mad demoniac mirth.

For a while O'Donnell kept the lad and himself afloat. They were swept under the waves, and came up again, only to see larger waves rushing towards them; but through all, the surgeon never loosened his hold, until a tremendous billow, engulfing them both, tore the boy from his grasp.

With the horror of his dream upon him he awoke to hear a voice quite distinctly:

"Go to the hospital—go at once!"

The surgeon started up in bed, rubbing his eyes, and looked around. The candle was flickering faintly in its socket. Brian, with his ears pricked forward, had raised his head at his master's sudden movement.

Everything was quiet, but still those words were ringing in his ear:

"Go to the hospital—go at once!"

The tremendous peal of the bell overnight, and this sentence, seemed to be simultaneous.

That he was wanted at Guy's—wanted imperatively—came to O'Donnell like an inspiration. Neither sense nor reason had anything to do with the conviction that roused him out of bed, and made him dress as speedily as possible, and grope his way down the staircase, Brian following.

He opened the front door, and passed out into the darkness. The rain was over, and the stars were shining as he pursued his way down Newport Market, and thence, winding in and out in a southeasterly direction, through Lincoln's Inn Fields and Old

Square to Chancery Lane, whence he proceeded to St Paul's.

Along the deserted streets he resolutely continued his walk. He did not know what he was going to Guy's for. Some instinct was urging him on, and he neither strove to combat nor control it. Only once did the thought of turning back cross his mind, and that was at the archway leading into Old Square. There he had paused for a moment, asking himself whether he were not gone stark, staring mad; but Guy's seemed preferable to the haunted house in Gerrard Street, and he walked resolutely on, determined to say, if any surprise were expressed at his appearance, that he had been sent for.

Sent for?—yea, truly; but by whom?

On through Cannon Street; on over London Bridge, where the lights flickered in the river, and the sullen splash of the water flowing beneath the arches, washing the stone piers, could be heard, now the human din was hushed and lulled to sleep. On, thinking of many things: of the days of his youth; of his dead brother; of his father's heavily encumbered estate; of the fortune his mother had vowed she would leave to some charity rather than to him, if he refused to marry according to her choice; of his wild life in London; of the terrible cry he had heard overnight—that unearthly wail which he could not drive from his memory even when he entered Guy's, and confronted the porter, who said:

"You have been sent for, sir; did you meet the messenger?"

Like one in a dream, Hertford O'Donnell heard him; like one in a dream, also, he asked what was the matter.

"Bad accident, sir; fire; fell off a balcony—unsafe—old building. Mother and child—a son; child with compound fracture of thigh."

This, the joint information of porter and house-surgeon, mingled together, and made a boom in Mr. O'Donnell's ears like the sound of the sea breaking on a shingly shore.

Only one sentence he understood properly—"Immediate amputation necessary." At this point he grew cool; he was the careful, cautious, successful surgeon, in a moment.

"The child you say?" he answered. "Let me see him."

The Guy's Hospital of today may be different to the Guy's Hertford O'Donnell knew so well. Railways have, I believe, swept away the old operating room; railways may have changed the position of the former accident ward, to reach which, in the days of which I am writing, the two surgeons had to pass a staircase leading to the upper stories.

On the lower step of this staircase, partially in shadow, Hertford O'Donnell beheld, as he came forward, an old woman seated.

An old woman with streaming grey hair, with attenuated arms, with head bowed forward, with scanty clothing, with bare feet; who never looked up at their approach, but sat unnoticing, shaking her head and wringing her hands in an extremity of despair.

"Who is that?" asked Mr. O'Donnell, almost involuntarily.

"Who is what?" demanded his companion.

"That—that woman," was the reply.

"What woman?"

"There—are you blind?—seated on the bottom step of the staircase. What is she doing?" persisted Mr. O'Donnell.

"There is no woman near us," his companion answered, looking at the rising surgeon very much as though he suspected him of seeing double.

"No woman!" scoffed Hertford. "Do you expect me to disbelieve the evidence of my own eyes?" and he walked up to the figure, meaning to touch it.

But as he assayed to do so, the woman seemed to rise in the

air and float away, with her arms stretched high up over her head, uttering such a wail of pain, and agony, and distress, as caused the Irishman's blood to curdle.

"My God! Did you hear that?" he said to his companion.

"What?" was the reply.

Then, although he knew the sound had fallen on deaf ears, he answered:

"The wail of the Banshee! Some of my people are doomed!"

"I trust not," answered the house-surgeon, who had an idea, nevertheless, that Hertford O'Donnell's Banshee lived in a whisky bottle, and would at some remote day make an end to the rising and clever operator.

With nerves utterly shaken, Mr. O'Donnell walked forward to the accident ward. There with his face shaded from the light, lay his patient—a young boy, with a compound fracture of the thigh.

In that ward, in the face of actual danger or pain capable of relief, the surgeon had never known faltering or fear; and now he carefully examined the injury, felt the pulse, inquired as to the treatment pursued, and ordered the sufferer to be carried to the operating room.

While he was looking out his instruments he heard the boy lying on the table murmur faintly:

"Tell her not to cry so—tell her not to cry."

"What is he talking about?" Hertford O'Donnell inquired.

"The nurse says he has been speaking about some woman crying ever since he came in—his mother, most likely," answered one of the attendants.

"He is delirious then?" observed the surgeon.

"No, sir," pleaded the boy, excitedly, "no; it is that woman—that woman with the grey hair. I saw her looking from the upper window before the balcony gave way. She has never left me since, and she won't be quiet, wringing her hands and crying."

"Can you see her now?" Hertford O'Donnell inquired, stepping to the side of the table. "Point out where she is."

Then the lad stretched forth a feeble finger in the direction of the door, where clearly, as he had seen her seated on the stairs, the surgeon saw a woman standing—a woman with grey hair and scanty clothing, and upstretched arms and bare feet.

"A word with you, sir," O'Donnell said to the house-surgeon, drawing him back from the table. "I cannot perform this operation: send for some other person. I am ill; I am incapable."

"But," pleaded the other, "there is no time to get anyone else. We sent for Mr. West, before we troubled you, but he was out of town, and all the rest of the surgeons live so far away. Mortification may set in at any moment and—."

"Do you think you require to teach me my business?" was the reply. "I know the boy's life hangs on a thread, and that is the very reason I cannot operate. I am not fit for it. I tell you I have seen tonight that which unnerves me utterly. My hand is not steady. Send for someone else without delay. Say I am ill—dead!—what you please. Heavens! There she is again, right over the boy! Do you hear her?" and Hertford O'Donnell fell fainting on the floor.

How long he lay in that death-like swoon I cannot say; but when he returned to consciousness, the principal physician of Guy's was standing beside him in the cold grey light of the Christmas morning.

"The boy?" murmured O'Donnell, faintly.

"Now, my dear fellow, keep yourself quiet," was the reply.

"The boy?" he repeated, irritably. "Who operated?"

"No one," Dr. Lanson answered. "It would have been useless cruelty. Mortification had set in and—"

Hertford O'Donnell turned his face to the wall, and his friend could not see it.

"Do not distress yourself," went on the physician, kindly. "Allington says he could not have survived the operation in any case. He was quite delirious from the first, raving about a woman with grey hair and—"

"I know," Hertford O'Donnell interrupted; "and the boy had a mother, they told me, or I dreamt it."

"Yes, she was bruised and shaken, but not seriously injured."

"Has she blue eyes and fair hair—fair hair all rippling and wavy? Is she white as a lily, with just a faint flush of color in her cheek? Is she young and trusting and innocent? No; I am wandering. She must be nearly thirty now. Go, for God's sake, and tell me if you can find a woman you could imagine having once been a girl such as I describe."

"Irish?" asked the doctor; and O'Donnell made a gesture of assent.

"It is she then," was the reply, "a woman with the face of an angel."

"A woman who should have been my wife," the surgeon answered; "whose child was my son."

"Lord help you!" ejaculated the doctor. Then Hertford O'Donnell raised himself from the sofa where they had laid him, and told his companion the story of his life—how there had been a bitter feud between his people and her people—how they were divided by old animosities and by difference of religion—how they had met by stealth, and exchanged rings and vows, all for naught—how his family had insulted hers, so that her father, wishful for her to marry a kinsman of his own, bore her off to a far-away land, and made her write him a letter of eternal farewell—how his own parents had kept all knowledge of the quarrel from him till she was utterly beyond his reach—how they had vowed to discard him unless he agreed to marry according to their wishes— how he left home, and came to London, and sought his fortune. All this Hertford O'Donnell repeated; and when he had finished, the bells were ringing for morning service— ringing loudly, ringing joyfully, "Peace on earth, goodwill towards men."

But there was little peace that morning for Hertford O'Donnell. He had to look on the face of his dead son, wherein he beheld, as though reflected, the face of the boy in his dream.

Afterwards, stealthily he followed his friend, and beheld, with her eyes closed, her cheeks pale and pinched, her hair thinner but still falling like a veil over her, the love of his youth, the only woman he had ever loved devotedly and unselfishly.

There is little space left here to tell of how the two met at last—of how the stone of the years seemed suddenly rolled away from the tomb of their past, and their youth arose and returned to them, even amid their tears.

She had been true to him, through persecution, through contumely, through kindness, which was more trying; through shame, and grief, and poverty, she had been loyal to the lover of her youth; and before the New Year dawned there came a letter from Calgillan, saying that the Banshee's wail had been heard there, and praying Hertford, if he were still alive, to let bygones be bygones, in consideration of the long years of estrangement—the anguish and remorse of his afflicted parents.

More than that. Hertford O'Donnell, if a reckless man, was honorable; and so, on the Christmas Day when he was to have proposed for Miss Ingot, he went to that lady, and told her how he had wooed and won, in the years of his youth, one who after many days was miraculously restored to him; and from the hour in which he took her into his confidence, he never thought her either vulgar or foolish, but rather he paid homage to the woman who, when she had heard the whole tale repeated, said, simply,

"Ask her to come to me till you can claim her—and God bless you both!"

Index

Aghavoe, 23
Agony, screams of, 120
Aherlow, 53
Angel, tutelary, 27
Apparitions, 20

Baptism, 51, 52
Banshee, 130, 132, 133, 134, 135, 138-39, 140, 142
Bantry, 69
Ben Bulben, 63, 64
Bennebeola Mountains, 126

Cahir, 54
Calgillan, 121, 126, 132, 134, 142
Cape Clear, 76
Cappagh, 54, 56, 57
Carmelites, 11
Charms, 24, 28, 29, 53, 57
Chloroform, 119
Clonmel, 10
Connemara, 125
Cures, 26, 27
Crossmolina, 40
Curses, 63, 64

Day of Judgment, 123
Death Chamber, 12
Demons, 33
Devil, 30, 98-102, 104-107, 110-16, 117, 122
Divine Providence, 24
Dursey Island, 69
Dunluce, 133

Eri, five kingdoms of, 60

Fairy carriages, 124
Fairy-women, 24, 70
Field of Gold, 60
Foxford, 41

Galtee Mountains, 53
Ghosts, 15
Glengarrif, 69
Guy's Hospital, 119, 122, 123, 136, 138

Holy candles, 12, 13, 22
Horseshoes, charmed, 28-29

Knocknarea, 63

Magpie, talking, 35-36

Oil o' the hazel, 92
Operations, surgical, 119-21

Pooka, 69, 77
Phantoms, 21, 22, 130, 134

Rathrowen, 48
Ribbon, talismanic, 27
Rossamara, 78, 79, 81

St. Moroky, 97, 116-17
Skibbereen, 80, 81
Spirits, evil, 18, 21
Supernatural, Methodists and, 15

Will-o'-the-wisp, 118